UNTAMED

By

Jack Grisham

Punk ★ Hostage ★ Press

Editor
Iris Berry

Associate Editors
Melissa Elhardt
Dyanne Gilliam

Introduction
S.A. Griffin

Interior Design
Michele McDannold

Cover & Illustrations
Scott Aicher

Punk Hostage Press
Hollywood, USA
punkhostagepress.com

Other Works by Jack Grisham

An American Demon ~ ECW Press 2011

Untamed ~ Punk Hostage Press 2013

Code Blue: A Love Story ~ Limited Edition
Punk Hostage Press 2014

A Principle of Recovery ~ 2015

I Wish There Were Monsters ~ 2015

Code Blue: A Love Story ~ The Hide Under Your Mattress Edition
~ Punk Hostage Press 2020

Editor's Acknowledgments

There are many people Jack would like to thank, who without their love, support, friendship and generous contributions, this book would not be possible. In Jack's own words—"My hat is tipped."

Punk Hostage Press would like to thank S.A. Griffin for his powerful introduction. A. Razor and Michele McDannold for always being there. Monika Velvet, Richard Modiano and Dimitrie Monroe. All the writers at Punk Hostage Press. And Red Stodolski at Baroque Books for carrying the torch for us all—your spirit will always live-on at the corner of Hollywood and Las Palmas.

Scott Aicher for his incredible cover art and illustrations. For always being available and willing to help in every way possible, any time, day or night.

Last, but certainly not least, thank you to Jack Grisham for his generosity of spirit and all that he does for so many communities.

Iris Berry 2021

Introduction

Nothing could have prepared me for the symbiotic wonderland of creative rage and genius that was waiting for me in the mushrooming punk bomb exploding across Los Angeles when I arrived here from San Francisco and the East Bay in 1978.

Forty and more years up the road, and many lives later, we are still here, still standing in the fallout, still mixing it up. Survivors still raging and creating, and in our various ways, still demanding to be part of the conversation. Among them is Jack Grisham, one of the most gifted humans I have ever encountered. Whatever *it* is, Jack's got *it*– as the white-face front man for T.S.O.L. and various other bands, photographer, filmmaker, writer, hypnotist, raconteur and comic wit, Jack Grisham is a royal flush.

This second edition of Jack's collected stories weren't written in the midst of this invisible crisis from social space that is redefining us all as I write this, but they sure as hell feel like they could have been, for these are emergency stories from the inside. Stories of survival. Raw and unbound reality for a reality fucked world, Jack's *Untamed* is a mission upriver in search of the hardcore heart of darkness.

As he is on stage, the same holds true on the page, Jack's delivery is honest, straight ahead, in your face and in your gut, taking no prisoners in the process. Frightening, fantastic and funny as hell, herein exists a violent rush of talking animals, street devils and fetish angels twisting with elements of a brawling Charles Bukowski, the macabre sensibility of Edgar Allen Poe and a dash of the dystopian Ray Bradbury. A blue-collar Twilight Zone straight out of Jack's imagination, *Untamed* is a journey into another dimension, built on fear and anger, lost in love and sadness, hanging onto threads of redemption at the end. Narratives and images that are bold and graphic, at times coalescing into surreal Odd Nerdrum fairytales. Tales cast with characters that are constant and clear, resulting in a collection of stories that place the reader inside each one, like a series of cinematic shorts, each unique world being viewed through the peep show lens of Quentin Tarantino or Frank Miller.

Untamed demands that once you buy the ticket, you're going to take the ride, and ride you will along a pandemic river, a viral reflection of an openly wounded world dipped in dysfunction, characters on the edge slamming against one another inside their exigencies trying hard to unfuck themselves as they fuck up, bent and howling, and bent on being human. All laid down on the page with great love and craft, without judgement or apology. No small feat.

S.A. Griffin
author of *Dreams Gone Mad With Hope*
editor of *Outlaw Bible of American Poetry*

I Love a Parade

On July 4th, Main Street became a traveling zoo. Great helium animals marched past the windows of his apartment. He resided on the third floor, which gave him a perfect angle to view the beasts of the parade. Today was his favorite day of the year. The crowds outside, had swelled so that he was almost able to feel their touch—their joy and Independence Day spirit climbing toward his heart—almost.

When was the last time that someone had knocked on his door? The manager of his apartment had been up some two months ago, but he wasn't sure if he could count that—you couldn't call a hand delivered "raise of rent" notice a friendly gesture. His phone hadn't rung either. The last call he received was from his ex-wife's new "friend." They had threatened a restraining order. He hadn't harassed her. He had wanted to get things straight. She was hard to get ahold of—didn't pick up her phone much, and the fact that she hadn't called him herself had given him some hope that maybe she still cared enough to not hurt him. Of course, that hope was gone now. Their relationship was no better than last year's streamers—colorful paper ropes, once so promising and beautiful...but then, swept into the street and dispatched to the trash.

He gazed through the window as a large Sponge Bob floated merrily by. He loved Bob's cartoons, although...it was surprising to see the sponge traveling down the street in an orderly fashion; the character was after all, a bit unruly. The thought made him smile.

He'd purchased a rope. It was coiled with care on the dining room table. It was a strong, nylon mountain climbing cord—expensive, but worth it, if it didn't break. He got down on his knees and secured one end of the rope around a stout table leg. This left him a length of about thirty-two feet, or the distance across the living room and two stories down—that is, if you were thinking about tossing it from the window.

He walked into the bedroom. The photographs from last year's vacation were lying on the floor. They were arranged in chronological order—a visual timeline. He'd imagined that if he could somehow walk down those frames—navigate the past, he could go back, bring her home and re-start their life together. It hadn't worked. While intoxicated, the plan had seemed like it could've been successful— or at least kind of successful, but in the morning, when sober, it was nonsense. He remembered thinking that if he had pictures of his childhood—from his first days in the world, that maybe he could have removed a shot or two and led an entirely different life. What were they using to take photos back then—Polaroids? Hmm—even in the 70s they were beginning to lose touch with slow, meaningful, relationships. Everyone wanted fast, instant gratification. Nobody worked on anything anymore, really tried before you cast something or…someone aside. Even the parade had gotten quicker. The long, winding, hang-on-to-the-tail-in-front chain was now skipping past as if it had somewhere else to go.

There was a marching band in the street below. He listened as the sound came close, hung for a verse or two and then, hurried on before the chorus.

He removed his clothes and considered himself in the mirror. He was tall—what some might call handsome, and his hair was still full and a dark summer blond. Yes, he was still attractive, but he was through. If someone had poked him—if they had gotten close enough, his comely outer shell would have shattered and the thick black gelatinous muck of defeat would have poured from inside. Shit. He hadn't thought of that. He hoped that when the time came he fell clean, without a cut. He'd hate to ruin the parade by raining muck on the spectators.

How'd it go bad anyway, his marriage to Katherine? He'd been gracious and kind. He was a good provider. He loved her more than anyone else ever could. She said he was angry—not with her—well...once or twice with her—but at everything. Come on, he had the complaints of any man; *why the fuck do they get that and I get this? What have I done to deserve the short end of the stick? 12 items, are you fucking kidding me?* Angry? No, not angry; he had a healthy willingness to not be pushed around—self-respect—pride.

He thought back to the day she'd left. He'd come home a touch late as usual—tired, but not overly so. He walked in—the same as he did every night, but this time he'd walked into the feeling of nothing. It was as if the house had died. There was no note, no explanation, and no mess. Everything was in its place, but no... something was missing—there, on the dresser...a hole, space— emptiness. What used to be there? He closed his eyes and the furnishings of the house disappeared. And then, a light in his mind began to flash—on and off, on and then off, brighter and brighter, until it became a small simple silver frame, four by six, cradling a photo of the two of them holding each other. It was gone. He'd never noticed how much power that photo had. The house was full of things that could be removed without him knowing. There were paintings on the walls—knick-knacks on the shelves; he'd never miss those. Even the TV in the living room could be gone for days without him taking note. The bed, sure, when he laid down, the shower-head, yes, of course—if he climbed under it and no water came out, but that photo, that innocuous little photo of the two of them holding each other, it was immediately missed. It was everything. It was the heart of this home.

He put his hand to his chest and wondered if the world would miss him, but he didn't wonder long. That small picture frame spot on the dresser, the one void of dust—Pledge-shiny waxed—held more power and created a deeper sense of longing than he ever could. He wouldn't be missed.

He walked naked into the living room. He checked the rope and then tied the loose end about his neck. As he did so he looked out the window and into the eyes of a large pink ape. The great beast reflected nothing of him or the room. He had already disappeared as far as this monster was concerned and, if it showed any interest at all, it was only the interest of an apartment hunter looking for a place to store its deflated self.

He moved to the window and opened it wide. Laughter and goodwill rushed from the street, scaled the building's walls, jumped the sill, and forced their rude notes upon him. Children, their joy-filled voices screaming. Where were they, his old candy-coated smiles and dirty-knee'd summer dreams?

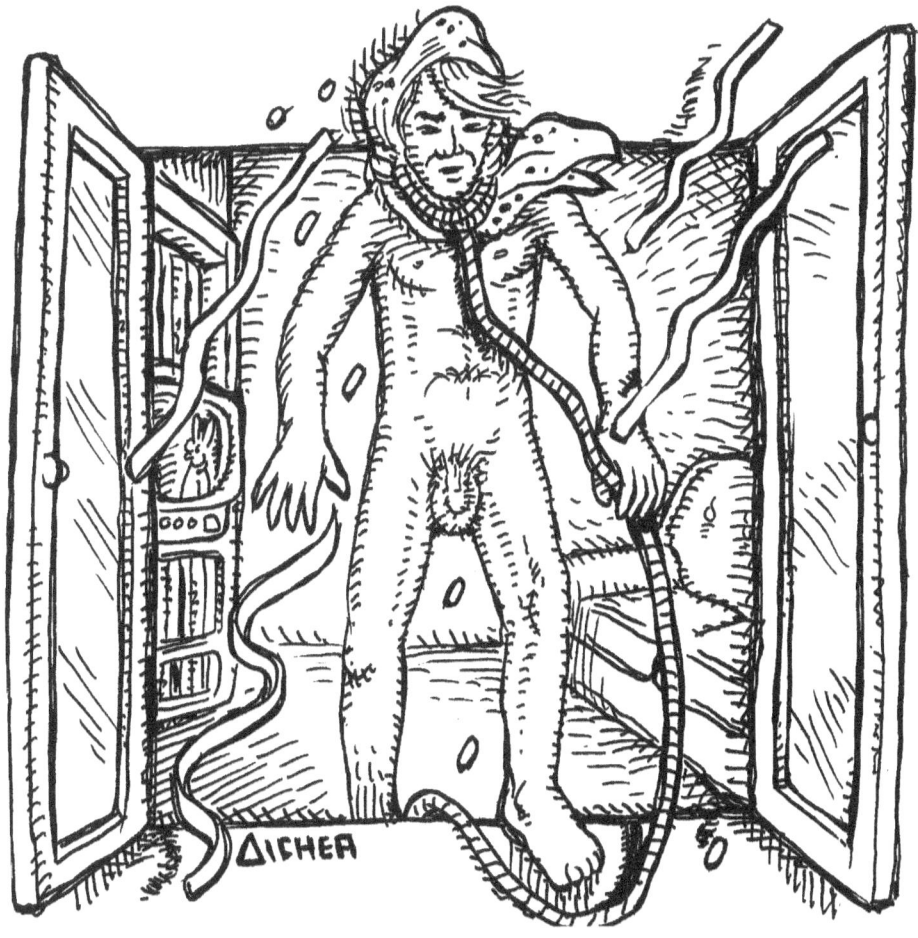

The rope was a touch rough around his neck so he untied it. He returned to the bedroom. A few of Katherine's things were left behind, including a scarf that he'd found in the back seat of his car. The scarf was a brilliant sky blue with dashes of yellow and green. Too bright for most, but when she wore it, the colors quailed beneath the blue of her eyes. It still carried her scent. He wondered why perfume stayed on clothes longer than it stayed on skin; and how, even when washed, like his button-down grey shirt had been, perfume could hang unfaithfully familiar as it clung to cloth. And maybe, there was that, his infidelity. But, he'd never been a one-woman-man. He needed more. He couldn't help that. She should have accepted him. He'd taken her tears and her monthly moods.

He tied her scarf around his neck. He was going to lose that "found nude" headline, but chafing was chafing, and there was no reason to be uncomfortable.

Wild horns brayed outside. A gang of clowns gathered below. They were reckless, crowding the street, dancing and honking, frightening the children.

He remembered a car ride with Katherine that had gone sour. What was she trying to say as he yelled at her—those tear-touched lips, moving without sound while the horns from the cars behind pushed his rage? They were stopped at a light. He'd jumped out, as any man would have. He walked back to set them straight. The crying pussy in the first car screamed as he was pulled through the window and beaten. And what of those other horn honking cunts—reversing in unison as he moved toward them? And yes, he shoved her. Yes, she hit hard enough to be knocked out. But, it was really just a push that had gotten out of control, the aggression of the moment, and if the window and the door jam hadn't been there to stop her head, she would've been fine. It wasn't his fault.

The clowns moved down the street.

He laid the rope across the scarf and pulled it tight. He climbed halfway through the window and worked his way into a sitting position on the sill. The breeze was cool. He sat, legs dangling over the crowd, and waited in vain for the telephone to ring. Katherine, had at times been telepathic, and although he was not in any great despair, she might reach out to say goodbye.

A float rounded the corner. It was a cartoon bear that he failed to recognize. It lumbered and danced in a non-threatening manner. "Bear," that's what Katherine had called him—her, "Big Bear." Yes, bears could be like this one—smiling, toddling cuteness down wide city streets or…they could be like other bears, like he was sometimes.

He let the rope drop.

It fell clean.

Leaning forward, his hands at his side, he paused. The parade had stalled. On the corner of Main and 12th a commotion ensued. The great happy bear had come undone. It was climbing into the sky—untethered, unemotional and unbowed. In the street below the One-hundred and Eleventh Street Band cranked up a tune. They were wonderful—their golden horns and orange plumed feather hats—a sea of color coaxing him on.

He smiled and pushed out from the sill.

And as the great happy bear rose—he fell.

He traveled the length of the rope and then his neck jerked and snapped with a loud pop.

The parade moved on.

Beautiful colored streamers dropped from above and draped his body. The crowd oblivious cheered. He bounced once or twice against the wall and came to rest. Hidden from the onlookers, his legs twitched and kicked in time with the band.

The Extraction

"She's a psychopath, a murdering psychopath and she's taken my heart!"

His office was small—a standard shrink setup, big couch, an overstuffed chair, boxes of Kleenex, and a wall covered with "here's-how-to-fix-their-heads" books. But there was nothing on those shelves to solve my problem. My heart had been violently, and with little regret, ripped from my chest.

"Jack, please," my therapist used his best sooth-the-savage-beast tones. "Please calm down."

"You don't get it, *Robert*." I was crying, and screaming at the same time. "She took my heart! My fucking heart!"

"Okay. I hear you. First off, that's a figure of speech; she doesn't *really* have your heart. You're emotionally attached to her and you're upset. You're hurting yes, but it's not physical."

I grabbed the front of my blood-soaked shirt and tore it open, exposing the jagged hole beneath. "Look at this! Am I lying? She cut me and she took it. She fucking took it."

"Jack, please. If she took your heart you'd be dead, but you're not dead, you're here screaming at me; you're alive, you're very much alive."

He was incapable of seeing it, but he worked on a sliding scale, and I was broke.

"Here," he said, as he handed me a large blue pill and a paper cup half filled with water. "Take this, please, it'll help."

I grabbed the pill from his hand and swallowed it dry. I wanted him to see it fall past the hole in my chest, but instead, it got caught in my throat and I was forced to drink—bitter, inner-city tap water.

"I can help you," he said, "but first you need to relax, calm down. I'll help you get it back."

"Don't humor me. And don't act like you can't see it." I gestured wildly at my shirt. "You know it's gone. Look! Look at it!"

"Jack, I believe that you believe, for now that's a start. Can you try to relax and listen to me, please?"

He got up and pulled the shades closed. I waited to stop breathing—this was agony.

"Sometimes," he said, "and I'm not saying that this is true in your case, but sometimes people can become so upset that they actually convince themselves that they're seeing and experiencing things that, well, just aren't so."

I ran my hand over the hole in my chest as he talked—I pulled at the collar of my bloody shirt. I gently tapped and pushed my fingers into the hollow as he pontificated. He was an idiot.

"Why don't you tell me how it happened then?" he asked. "Tell me *how* she took your heart."

I was losing a lot of blood, and I don't know if the pill he gave me was kicking in, but I figured that if I calmly laid out my story, minus the hysterics, he might believe me and take notice of the hole.

"It was last night," I said. "We were supposed to go out, but she said that she had homework to finish—math, she needed it done by tomorrow. I didn't trip on it; she is in school and a lot more conscientious than I'd ever been, so I believed her. I kicked it at my place for a bit, perved on some porn, got bored, and then I figured I'd surprise her with a visit—no problem. I told you she got that place in Long Beach, near the gay ghetto, right? Well, parking is a real bitch down there, so I cruised around until I found a spot—on Falcon—a couple blocks over from her place. It was a short walk, but along the way I got a taste of how a single girl might feel. I had to stroll past those boy bars on Broadway—had the leather cats calling me names and trying to get me to hang out for a drink. Anyway, I got to her house and knocked on the door—no answer. Well, I hadn't told her I was on my way, so I texted her and asked how it was going. She got right back to me, LOL about how she was lying around in the living room with her panties off as she studied. Well, now *I knew she was lying*, she wasn't home because I was knocking. The fucking bitch had no idea I was standing at her front door—so I broke in."

"What?" Dr. Robert was shocked. "Did you just say that you broke into her apartment?"

"No. I didn't *'break in'*; I took a screen off and went through the window. I didn't kick the fucking door down."

"You committed a crime, Jack."

"Yeah," I grabbed at my blood soaked shirt. "Well, I don't think *she's* going to be pressing charges, is she?"

The doctor sighed and waved his hand for more of the story. I threw him a disgusted don't-stop-me-again look.

"Her house was a mess—clothes and books all over the place. She's gorgeous, but she's a fucking slob—her car looks like a homeless camp. Anyway, I was quiet going in, just in case she *was* home and, if so, I was gonna pull one of those 'look-at-the-cute-burglar/boyfriend' things. But she wasn't there, so after a quick look around, I went through her things, or at least I started to, because when I got to her bedroom, there were rope ties out—one on each corner of the bed, with handcuffed leather attachments and a big dildo lying on the mattress. Now you know I got a bit of the kink running through me, but we've never fucked around like *that*, so unless she had something planned for later, this wasn't meant for me."

"Why didn't you just leave? You and I have talked about this before, Jack. You know she's unfaithful, always has been. You could've been arrested. What are you getting out of this?"

"I'M GETTING THE FUCKING TRUTH OUT OF IT!" I screamed, "I want to see her doing it. Every time I think I catch her doing something, there's always an explanation, always a reason that what I'm seeing isn't true."

"She admitted…"

"SHE NEVER ADMITTED ANYTHING! She cries and rolls those sad brown eyes at me—she's a witch, a psychopathic witch!"

"Jack?"

"No! You listen to me. I got a text as I was standing by the bed. It was her, asking me if I'd left home yet. I was quick. I wrote back 'no' and asked if she was done studying. She wrote back telling me that she was gonna take a nap and that the phone would be off for a bit, so I should wait to come over. You see, she always does that, always has a reason why she can't answer, and why I can't get a hold of her. So I throw a quick 'Yeah, no problem babe, I'm bummed I gotta wait, but let me know when you're up.'—I threw that last bit in because if she thought I went along too easily she'd get suspicious. So, I didn't have a real plan or anything, but I knew my car was cool, because like I said it was a couple blocks over. So I sat there, whimpered for a bit, and then tried to put a thought together."

"We've talked about this before, you taking a moment out— running the situation through your head—and then, maybe calling a friend, or myself; and at least leaving that very illegal situation."

"Yeah, and I probably could have. I was in deep, but I *was* calming down—having a real moment of clarity—realizing that I didn't need to deal with this shit, just like you've said. I *was* better than her, *and* better than this—but then I heard voices in the alley. It was her, and she was laughing, so I got inside the closet."

"What?" The doctor was taken aback.

"I would have climbed under the bed but it was full of boxes and shit, dirty clothes—shoes. The closet wasn't much better, but it was easier, and I figured if she needed something she'd just grab it off the floor. So there I was, standing in a crowd of empty coats and dresses, when I heard 'em come in—two people, as far as I could tell, her and some woman. It was real strange because I heard laughter, talking, and then silence, talking again, silence, like somebody was pressing the 'mute' button during their conversation. I was tripping, but then I realized that they must have been kissing. I couldn't see 'em, but the silence, followed by the talking, told me they were. Fuck, I wanted to break out and confront 'em right then—come out real Bruce Lee style—kicking and throwing blows, but not this time. Fortunately, I realized I had done that before, it didn't work."

"You've caught her with someone before?" the doctor said. "You never told me that."

"No! Fuck! I didn't say I *caught her! I've* never caught her, *but I've caught her* getting ready to do shit, and I broke in before she did it, so I didn't actually catch her."

"So, you haven't actually caught her being unfaithful."

"Fuck!" I yelled. "YOU FUCKING SOUND LIKE HER! NO, that's what I told you. *I needed evidence. I needed to catch her. That's why I stayed.*"

Dr. Robert gave me a disbelieving look that I verbally rolled right over. "I was good. I didn't yell out, watched my breathing, stayed calm and I waited—just like you've taught me."

"I never taught you that," the doctor said. "I taught you to leave."

He needed to be quiet.

"They screwed around in the kitchen a bit, her and whoever—and it started to look like I was gonna have to just come out and confront them, but then they walked into the bedroom. God, that *thing* she was kissing—who sounded like a woman, it didn't look like one. I peeped out through the closet door—just a touch, a crack. The bitch had a fucking chain wallet, and Levi's cuffed over her boots. I'm telling you, a real nasty-looking thing with dreadlocked dirty blonde hair hanging to her waist. She had her back to me, and my girl had her arms thrown around the bitch's neck like some lesbian perfume ad—her face buried in what I assumed to be this thing's tits. I wouldn't be surprised if that big bitch had 'em taped down or whacked off or whatever—I mean, for all intents and purposes, this could have been a soft-assed ugly boy. I stayed quiet, and they kissed. That big thing laid my chick down on the bed. My girl was pulling and stroking those rope ties as they made out—like she was stroking a cock or something. Well, then they separated—broke it off—and the big girl got up and started taking off her clothes—

folding them actually, which was kind of funny because the floor was littered with piles of used shirts and shit. It would have made more sense if she'd just tossed her crap on the ground. She took off her pants and T-shirt, and then she pulled off this sports bra and these big britches—more like a man's BVD's—bigger than mine. Then she stands there, naked, with that nasty-looking wig hair, and she watches my girl as *she* begins taking off *her* things and throwing them on the floor."

"How far were you going to let this go?" The doctor asked.

"I told you, Doc, all the way. I had to see it. I *was* a bit scared, wondering if I could physically take on that big bitch when I came out of the closet—but I didn't need to worry about that. My girl had pulled off all her things and then she started squirming and wiggling around on that bed like a viper, nesting on the covers, and that big old dyke, she was rubbing that nasty snatch of hers as she watched my girl move. And then Doc, my girl holds out a hand, reaching for that mannish thing, and she grabs onto her and with *crazy strength*, my chick pulled that bitch down on the bed and flipped her over. So now she's lying on her back with my girl on top, straddling her, holding her down. Fuck, that big girl wasn't pretty at all, hell, she wasn't even cute—more like a beast than a girl—and I was almost jealous that my chick was about to have sex with her but then I remembered that unless that dyke had an 8-inch clit there wasn't any real fucking going on—do you think that's weird?"

"What?" Dr. Robert was confused. "Do I think what's weird?"

"Do you think it's weird that, I don't really think it's cheating because she doesn't have a cock?"

"I don't get it. What are you saying? Are you saying she's not cheating on you?"

"No. I don't know. Maybe, I just use that to lessen the pain." I touched the hole in my chest, "Not that it helps much."

"Anyway, so my girl grabs one of those ties and locks that dyke's right arm up, and then the left arm, and then each leg. I thought the ropes were for my chick. When my girl had her all tied up, she started sliding on her, grinding her cunt against her like she's sitting on a cock, riding her, and then she reaches down on the side of the bed, grabs a big black hood and pulls it over that big girl's head. That dyke didn't like it—she was jerking around, trying to get away, struggling hard, but then my girl leaned forward and said, *'You go quiet now.'* Just like that, and that big old bitch just laid her head back—relaxed and silent—like an animal hypnotized into sleep—like some Crocodile Dundee bullshit."

"God damn it, Jack, that's enough. I told you before; *it's a waste of my time and yours for you to keep coming in here with these crazy tales…*"

"No, please, Robert, listen to me. Please, I'm not lying. Let me finish." And in the good doctor's favor, I might have lied to him once or twice, but not this time.

"I know it sounds crazy, but she did it. And that big girl looked like she was knocked out—lying there, not moving. I'm wondering if she's even breathing, and then, out of nowhere, my girl cocked her arm back and punched that bitch in the face—an undefended shot that I know did damage. And then she threw another—blow after blow. She was beating that girl of hers with more fury than I'd ever seen and she was yelling, screaming, *'I fucking hate you! I hate you!'* It was sickening. I was terrified. She was beating on her— screaming, crying, pounding, on that big girl who just laid there knocked out, taking hit after hit, and then I saw the blood seeping from under the hood, staining the bed, covering my girl's hands, and I couldn't take it anymore. I broke from the closet and I screamed: STOP IT! FUCKING, STOP IT!"

"My girl froze mid-punch—arm pulled back like a cocked

trigger flash—a beautiful vicious beast suspended at bay. And then she turned on me with eyes driven by checked fury, and she smiled—a great winter-snow smile that sent waves of perfumed terror rippling across my soul. And then, she whispered to me the same line she'd whispered before, *'You go quiet now,'* and I did. I stood there, rooted to the floor, arms to my side, eyes open, fully aware—unable to move."

"So, what happened?" The doctor asked, a touch of belief had crept into his voice. "What did she do then?"

"She looked happy to see me—like she wasn't doing anything wrong at all. Her smile became the pleasure of a afternoon summer walk, and with a two-lovers-cuddled-at-home grin she reached down and lovingly squeezed my cock and said, *'Do you like watching me? You're a naughty little boy aren't you?'* If only I had sensation to react to her words, you'd have seen the fear run through my eyes. She was not human."

"She slid her hand up my body, like a child sailing a dream ship on a nighttime river, and then she docked her fingers at my lips and told me to wait—as though I had choice. I stood there and watched as she untied her lover. She removed the hood from the big girl—whose face was swollen and colored red with blood. But the big dyke didn't move—leaving me to wonder if she *was* dead, but she wasn't. With a soft-mouthed word from my girl, her beaten lover arose and dressed herself in trancelike, mechanical-girl movements. With abused precision she donned her clothes and then walked from the room. I was still held in state so I couldn't see the exchange as my girl followed her out, but I heard the front door close and her returning footsteps."

"She stood before me. *'What am I to do with you?'* she asked—still holding that sweet lover's tone. *'You are a naughty one, but I like naughty, although…you did stop my fun.'*"

"She grabbed me by the collar of my shirt—her dainty hand wrapped, cuddled in the cloth, and then she pulled me toward the bed. I followed. She spun me 'round and then unbuttoned my pants, sliding them off my hips and kneeling before me—a submissive pose but one more akin to eating the soft belly of a kill than it was to kneeling before her master. She put her hands on my ass and I felt her fingernails cutting deep into my flesh—although there was no pain accompanying their assault. It was as if my body was made of wax, a man-doll for her to play with. I felt myself get hard and then she opened her mouth and swallowed me deep, but I received no pleasure from her, no sensation at her touch. It was just wet and

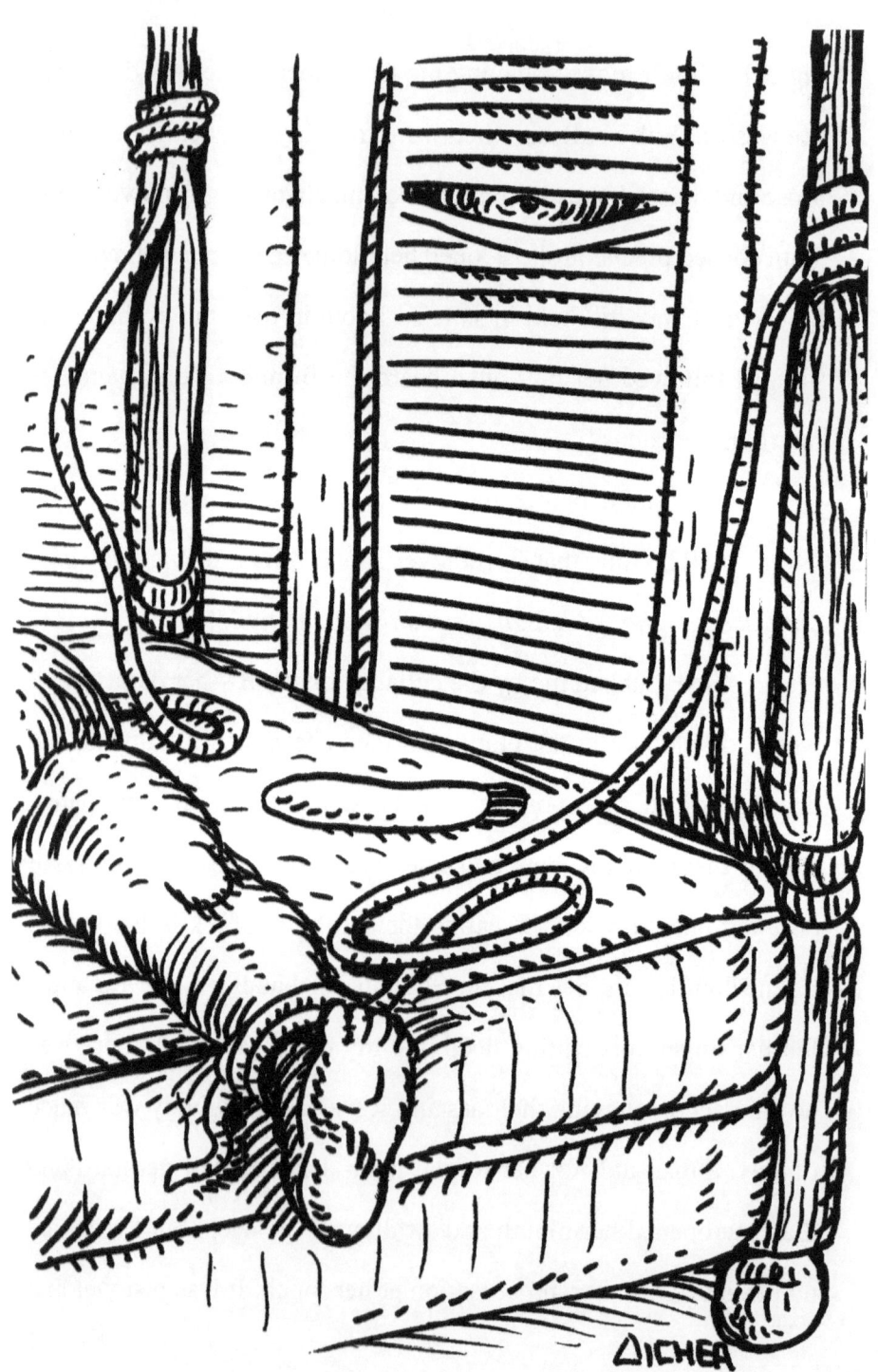

cold, almost as if I was exposed to the outside—a winter mouth devoid of warmth. She stood, pulled my shirt over my head, and pushed me backwards onto the bed that was recently vacated by her lover. She pulled off my shoes, my pants, and then reused the ties on me. I was now straddled on my back, tied to the bed, with my cock erect to her will."

"Jack?" the doctor's voice was soft, almost reverent, "You're bleeding." He pointed at my shirt.

"Yes," I said. "I know."

I looked at him with fatal eyes—my story not quite finished.

"She stepped up onto the bed, stood with her bare feet on the mattress, and looked down upon me. From where I lay she was a giantess, legs spread, towering over me. She touched herself, her fingers sensually caressing the outside of her cunt. I was not a man to her. I was property waiting to be scented. And then she squatted over me and placed my hard unfeeling cock inside. I wasn't conscious of any release, but after a short while of her ministrations she seemed satisfied, completed. She stayed squat—inhaling deeply, sucking her stomach in, drawing the semen up into her womb and rubbing her pelvic mound in wide circular moves as she repeated my name."

"Did she want a child?" the doctor asked. "Had you talked

about it, was it discussed before?"

"No," I said. "She'd mentioned a family, but there were no real plans. She climbed off me and then lay at my side—again, soft and loving, nestled against my skin. It was a posture she'd assumed many times, but that was before I knew what she was."

"What do you mean?" he asked. "What was she?"

"She was a witch. She placed trances and spells, wove lies with truth, love with selfishness. Her cunt held the comfort of evening slumbers and her kiss, like an early morning mist drifting upon an ocean of forgetfulness. This was a woman who would've been fuel for a fire—an accelerant on a medieval pyre."

"She put her lips to my forehead, and spoke: *'I hate myself for wanting her.'* She gestured outside, in what I took as the general direction of her beaten lover. *'She means nothing to me; it's you that I love. That woman, and the others I've had who are like her, they're just shadows of me, totems of my sexuality that I rape and deface.'*"

"I couldn't protest, or argue with her. I was still trapped in that space of evil compliance."

"*'I can't stay with you now—not after you've seen this, and I'm going to kill this child before he's born.'* She tenderly touched her stomach. *'His death will be my punishment—the promise of you that I've ripped from my life.'* She was tracing her fingers over my heart as she spoke. I could feel her tugging at my skin, the sensation of a loose nail pulled from a finger, or the torn head of a blister off your foot. Tears filled my eyes. I didn't understand. If I was so important to her, caused her so much pain, how could she do this? How could she hurt me?"

"'You were everything to me," she said, "and you promised me your heart—your love forever.'"

"And I *had* done that. I promised that I'd love her, and my heart was hers."

"'I'm taking what you owe me,' she purred, *'I'm taking what's mine, and then I'm leaving.'"*

I could say nothing.

"It was then that my body dipped below the surface, like an old wooden coaster plunging helplessly toward the ground. I felt my heart rise from my chest and then I blacked out. When I came to, the room was empty. I was lying on the floor of her now-vacant place and I was without a heart. She was gone."

"It's frightening to know that the organ that drives blood through your veins, the engine of life that tirelessly pumps throughout the day, can be cut from your body, and you can still exist."

"As you might imagine, I was turned away from the emergency room. That was my first stop after I wandered dazed from her apartment to my car. The doctors there couldn't see the problem. They were busy and in no mood to listen, so I came to you. I know you can't help me. You can't replace what she took, but maybe now you can acknowledge the hole, see how the blood refuses to dry on my shirt, and watch how I live devoid of its presence."

"Jack, there must be something I can do," the doctor said.

"You could kill her," I laughed, only half joking. "But if I were you, I'd be afraid that maybe one day she might come here with a different tale, a twist on what I just told you, a gleam in her eye as she sits on your sofa and makes you feel warm and loved."

"She'd never do that," he said.

"Of course she would." I said. "You've helped me. And now you believe that she did this to me. You know I love her and a true witch can't suffer a love to live."

I leaned back on his sofa. I was tired, worn down and through.

"Jack?" He spoke in a kind voice. "I'm afraid your time is up."

"Yeah," I said, "I know."

I took one last breath as the hole in my chest devoured me.

Untamed

Animals can be tamed, so can men, but underneath the groomed fur or the business suit, the bejeweled collar or that perfect tie—fragilely held in place, lives the true nature of the beast. Sometimes this nature can be held down long enough to drown under the socialized weight of the modern world, but at other times the animal within lies fiercely kicking beneath the skin—waiting for a chance to surface and let it's real life begin.

The teen Boy was wild and dangerous, unstable, the kind of boy who might do anything in a crowd. The Outsider pulled his jacket closed and one-hand checked his wallet. He hoped there weren't more of these boys.

"Hey man, you got some change?" The wild boy's eyes drifted to the recently covered wallet pocket.

"No…uh, I don't," the Outsider nervously rattled. "I only have plastic." He was polite, but dishonest.

"You sure you don't have something?" the boy asked as he monkey-cocked his head to the side. The boy was tall and pale—greasy jet-black hair cruised the collar of his leather jacket. He wore a white T-shirt and straight-legged Levi's cuffed over boots—'50s motorcycle wild-boy look—the kind of Marlon Brando cool that the Outsider wished he could summon up on a Friday night.

"How 'bout a ride then?" the boy asked. "I heard keys. You

got a car, yeah?"

The Outsider had a car. He also had a wife, two children, a large mortgage, and a small paying job. The Outsider had lots of things.

"Come on man," the boy said, "it ain't far. I missed the fucking bus."

The Outsider could have easily brushed the boy off and limp-dicked his way to the car, but for some reason he paused, as if something instinctual, yet foreign, had crawled out from his soul and gently wrapped itself around his legs…he was ashamed to say no to the boy.

"Okay, I guess so. If it's not too far." He submissively led the boy toward the car.

The wild boy was cool. He climbed in and leaned back against the worn leather seat. It was one of the few new-car options that the Outsider didn't take a pass on—leather had seemed right. The boy fooled with the window button as the Outsider looked down and unconsciously admired the outline of the boy's cock through his pants. It looked large, well shaped, and heavy. The Outsider had a cock once. When he was a teen, he had a real nice piece. He was proud of the way it stood forth in the shower, how it hung down between his legs as he walked, but not any more. He couldn't remember the last time he felt proud—or hard. He reached down and tried to adjust what he had left—the beige poly-cotton blend of his slacks city-boy whimpered, then laid still.

"Cool car man," the boy said. "What's it cost, a car like this? You must have some job, huh?"

The Outsider felt slightly buoyed by the boy's praise of his mid-priced, mist grey sedan—until he spotted a grape juice stain and the gummed end of a Zwieback cookie on the seat. *Fucking Sheila, I told her not to let the kids eat in the car...*

The boy rolled with his praise. "Yeah, real cool ride. You must have a good job—you a lawyer or something?"

The Outsider nodded his head with a move that could easily be mistaken for a casual yes. It was another lie. The Outsider was a process server. The car was an overpriced piece of shit.

"Hey, pull over here," the boy pointed to a run-down corner market. "I gotta get me something."

The Outsider didn't remember any such store near his home, and on second glance, he realized that, without paying attention, he had driven the boy farther and deeper into an area that the Outsider had no business being in. It was certainly nowhere he'd drift to on his own. He pulled to the curb. The boy jumped out without shutting the door. The Outsider called after him in a weak voice, "Hey, not too long, huh?"

There were black street corner animals lounging in twos and threes against the faded paint walls of the building. The Outsider had heard of these people—shiftless, lazy, drug dealers all, they weren't to be trusted. This was no place to be alone. The Outsider leaned over and just to be safe, pulled the door closed. He felt unprotected, vulnerable, almost as if something might come along and rip his arm off. He turned the radio on, but for some reason the reception was poor. It sounded distant—far off—even the commercials that were normally twice as loud as the soft adult-oriented pop that he enjoyed seemed garbled and washed out. He wished the boy would return. He felt safe in his presence. The Outsider, at six-foot-four, two hundred and thirty pounds, was much larger and stronger than the boy, but the Outsider felt small. His thoughts drifted to the wife he had at home…

Sheila had always thought him weak. She never came right out and said it, but it was there—tucked neatly inside her wifely tones. She thought she could've done better. One night he caught her sizing him up as they drove to the market. She looked disappointed as she ran her buyer's-remorse eyes over his bargain goods—his thinning hair and softening gut of a somewhat past-the-expiration-date man. He watched as she shook off the thought of him, and turned her mind toward what he knew was check-stand Tom—the big-shot grocery store manager, with a full head of hair and a worked out ass. He saw her face break into that slow, soft, upturned, nasty little grin that meant she was mind-fucking that overgrown box boy. That's okay. He knew what she was doing, and he had a fantasy of his own—a late-night store run that didn't work out so well for the check-out man—a fantasy that ended with big Tom knocked out and burbling in the Outsider's piss. But, of course, it was just a fantasy. The one time he'd met Tom's eyes across the checkout counter—even though the manager was store-bought-customer-polite—the Outsider had

turned from his glance. It was as if Tom could read his thoughts and

he was about to be pummeled and dropped for his insolence…

The car door re-opened and the wild boy jumped in with a
six-pack of cold beer and an even cooler grin of satisfaction.

"Come on, hit it!" the boy ordered.

The Outsider, without looking, wildly accelerated, forcing
the car into traffic.

"You gotta love those little yellow motherfuckers. Ha! What
the fuck did he think he was gonna do? Standing up all shit like
that." The boy was loud—babbling disjointed commentary on what
might have been some sort of violent exchange. His voice rose into a
sing-songy Asian squeal. "You're breeding on me! You're breeding
on me!"

The boy laughed—great white teeth bared—reflecting the
hard flesh of his lips—head thrown back against the seat. There were
fresh cuts on the boy's knuckles—wet red tears on Levi caressing
fingers. The Outsider could smell the blood. It thrilled him. He was
fascinated by the unrepentant naughtiness of the boy's ragged skin.

The instinctual feeling that had crept from within began
to overtake the tamed man. The boy back-knuckled his cut hand

beneath the Outsider's nose, teasing him, before dragging it slowly across the man's cheek—marking him with scent. The Outsider leaned into it and without thought, kitten-purred tragically against the boy's torn flesh—bonding with the more experienced male. As the boy pulled away, the Outsider grabbed his arm, and drew the boy's fingers toward his mouth. He reached out with his tongue and licked the blood from the wild boy's hand.

The boy was pleased.

"Ha! Tastes good, huh? Too bad it's mine. Never hit a fucker in the mouth—dirty fucking teeth, man. It's fun to feel 'em break, but fuck can they cut ya—dirty fucking teeth," the boy laughed as he spoke.

The Outsider was impatient. He wanted in on the action and

like a hungry whelp, he barked at the boy. "What happened?" the Outsider demanded. The boy swung heavy, pushing the question down with raised body and posture aggressive. The Outsider backed away, symbolically rolled over in his seat and spoke slowly with proper respect.

"I mean, are you okay?"

The boy cut the Outsider slack he hadn't yet earned.

"We needed beverages, man," the boy mimicked a low, drugged-out, stoner voice, from a popular film that the Outsider had once watched with his wife. *He remembered Sheila putting up a stink about the film's foul language and its sexual innuendo—fuck her.* The boy held up a beer. He took a long, slow, jungle-pull off the suds, and then he passed the half emptied can to the Outsider, who greedily put his mouth over the tombstone opening, swallowing the boy's scent, and chasing it down with cold malt.

"He fucking tried to stop me, dude. I'm walking out with a couple of cold beers and all five-foot-two of grass-hoppin' shit comes 'round the counter acting all Kung-Fu bad," the boy slid back to the sing-songy yellow jive. "Hey man, you got pay! You got pay!"

"When he grabbed for the beer I swung it up and hit him in the face with it—tee'd off on that big ole fucking head of his—

knocked his ass out."

"Really?" asked the Outsider.

"*Yeah, really.*" The Boy held up his cut hand. "What the fuck?" He flung blood on the Outsider's face. "You think I'm fuckin' with you?"

"No, I just…"

"Fuckin' A, man. Right in the fucking mouth!"

The Outsider wished he could have seen it, or better yet, maybe *he* could have given the little yellow man a kick—hit him when he was down, maybe a bit more. He wondered what it was like to beat someone.

"I got cash, too." The boy held up a wad of crumpled bills. "I mean, fuck, with him all sleeping on the job and everything, there ain't no sense not getting in that register and teaching him a lesson for being so fuckin' lazy." The boy fanned the cash like a child waving an exemplary school report.

"Gas money, baby!" He held out a twenty to the Outsider. "Go ahead, take it man."

The Outsider reached, a virgin, toward the ill-gotten bill.

"Come on," the boy coaxed. "It's cool."

The Outsider took the money. It felt good to be part of.

* * * * * * * * * * *

The pair slow-cruised the town—the boy pointing out dangers and easy meats, things to avoid and places to hide. The Outsider was hungry for knowledge—intent as he drove. This was a city he was unfamiliar with; a world he knew existed but he knew not the breadth and the deep colors of the land. As the boy spoke, the Outsider grew. His hips became heavy. His shoulders forward rolled.

"This is Felix's place." The boy pointed to an alley separating two tenement buildings. "Gave me my first cut, that nasty fucker." He pulled up his shirt displaying a long jagged scar running across the length of his stomach. "He took my cash and did me," the boy giggled. The Outsider deep inhaled the air as he strained to catch a whiff of Felix's scent—a cut like that was serious, nothing to laugh about.

The boy looked the Outsider over, appraised his size and possible worth, and then he flashed an idea. "Pull over here." The boy directed the Outsider to a small dirty parking lot. "We're gonna do this. He don't know you."

The wild boy laid out his plan—a way in, but as far as the Outsider could see, no reasonable way out—a roll-up attack, and he was bait.

"Felix will never see you coming—no offense man, but you look like a stupid fuck. With that jacket and tie, you're just one more coked-out junior exec hoping for a downtown score."

The Outsider nodded his head in agreement.

He imagined the broken bones and body parts invisibly strewn about the lair of Felix. It was a dangerous place. The building on the right—a great rock cliff, to the left, a brick wall running from the floor of the city and into the stars. Steam and a gutter stench of river drifted from the mouth of the alley—the haze of an inner city plain. The Outsider entered, feigning preoccupation—a human waterbuck searching for sweeter grass in the alley. Felix was there. The Outsider could feel the heavy weight of his presence; the polyester wrapped crocodile, fat and dangerous, leaning against the hard alley wall.

"You looking for something, bitch?" It was a deep Latin hiss of voice.

Felix moved toward the center of the alley—strong-coiled action, low smooth vicious cool. The Outsider felt his balls drop. He caught the wicked scent of abused flesh and alcohol-raped breath. Felix was beautiful. He was scarred and used, chewed up by the city, yes, but before it could swallow him, he'd been spit back as spun hard survivor into the street. His face was cut brown dirt. His eyes, blue Cadillac Deville, and in his mouth, the glint of spit-shined gold. He hypnotized the Outsider.

"I said you looking for something?"

"Coke?" The Outsider stammered—more question than request—he played his part well. Felix wide-smiled across the alley. "I ain't even gonna ask if you're a cop—you're too stupid to be a cop and there ain't no sense in selling what I ain't got, and you ain't getting. Now why don't you reach in those fucking pockets and dump your shit on the ground."

The Outsider moved further into the darkness. Felix followed—his mind salivating on his midafternoon snack of credit cards, wallet, and watch.

"I said drop your shit, bitch."

Felix flashed his claws—a blade, pulled from the air, clicked and switched in his hand.

The wild boy crept behind—quiet, jungle-stealth calm— advancing on Felix. In his hands, he held a board—a large cast-off piece of sharp alley trash. Felix saw him not. The Outsider reached into his pockets as if to surrender his worth.

"Yeah, dat's right, big man. You got nowheres to go, and maybe ole Felix is gonna give you something to suck on while you're here." Felix grabbed his crotch. "Shit, you prolly didn't even come down for blow; you come down here to get on my shit."

As he pulled foul-breath close to the Outsider, the wild boy struck—a flash lightening slash to the side of Felix's head. The monster staggered, blindly slow-danced toward his death. The boy swung again. The blow landed squarely on the brute's face—crushing bone, splitting flesh. His knife fell flaccid to the street. His skull crushed. His cock withered in his pants. Felix became one with the ground. The boy dragged the body behind a dumpster. He turned and offered the wooden tool to the Outsider.

"Here you go, get some. Be quick."

The Outsider grabbed the board and poked the body with it. The decaying flesh of the beast gave in and out—manipulated breath from the Outsider's touch.

"Go on," the wild boy urged. "What are you waiting for? Hit the fucker. We gotta get out of here."

The Outsider returned the weapon. "I can't," he said.

"What? Why not?"

"I'm not angry, I'd like to hit him—it seems like the right thing to do, but I'm not angry."

"Angry at what?" the boy asked, "I don't get it." He pointed to the body. "How you gonna be mad at that? There's him and you, me, those people out there," the boy gestured to the street. "We do what we do. It's got nothing to do with 'anger.' What the fuck you talking about?"

The Outsider was on the verge of understanding. The boy's simple, street animal logic walked along the edges of a mind made soft by the teachings of weak men—men who thought they were above something, created by something, to be more than man.

The boy questioned the corpse: "Who's cut now, huh,

fucker?"

The Outsider reached for the plank, but again, hesitation.

"That's okay man," the boy dropped the weapon to the ground. "You'll get a taste for it soon enough." The wild boy rifled Felix's pockets. He scored a small bag of dope and a few large bills. He stepped away with a parting kick. "Come on, man. We gotta go." He moved toward the car.

The Outsider walked after the boy, but then…he had a pure thought. He turned back and stomped on the body. It was a quick, non-remorseful, non-enlightened move—instinctual and soulful. He crouched and then rose with one of Felix's teeth—the spit-shined gold incisor.

The Outsider held the tooth in his palm and smiled a once man smile. He placed the tooth in his pocket, and loped after the boy.

* * * * * * * * * * *

They drove the Interstate a few short exits from downtown. Destination, the boy's place—a house he shared with others of his kind.

The neighborhood was a maze of burned-out cars, abandoned sofas, refrigerators, and trash. Toys—stuffed animals, some partially dismembered, were orphaned on the street. The few small children the Outsider had seen looked feral and he wondered if the plush toys were traps to weed out the weak. The wild boy's place was a single-story nondescript, inner-city tract house that might once have been yellow. There was a used-to-be lawn, chain-link fence, and a wheel-less truck on blocks in the drive. A large dog—vicious and snarling, was chained to a tree in the yard. The boy silenced the cur with a well-aimed kick. They walked up the cracked sidewalk to the house. The Outsider moved differently now—lower, more saunter, less stroll. He followed the boy up to the porch and stood quietly as the boy pounded on the door. The Outsider reached above his head to a wooded crossbeam. He pulled himself up, off the rough rotten boards, and without disdain he took in the broken windows, rusted chairs and torn yellow-white pull-down shades—cheap circus decor.

"You stand behind me, when we go in. You'd probably get beat down if you walked in first—and keep your fucking mouth shut, these guys don't like new things, and you're real new."

The boy knocked six times—three, and then three again, in quick succession—a tribal drum code for "friendly and entering." The door was cracked open from inside and the boy pushed his way into the darkness. The Outsider placed his hand on the small of the wild boy's back and followed him through.

The inside of the house was dark and warm. There was nothing on the walls, and the furniture—or what passed for furniture, were cast off sofas that looked pulled in from the street. They were burrowed in—nested on. There were no chairs. In the air, a musty odor of wet fur and urine. It was not a place the Outsider would have normally felt comfortable in, and yet, here he was. The scent was not unpleasing to whom he was now becoming—a new man. There were five large males in the room—great beasts in various stages of undress and agitation—prowling; their well-hung energy spoke jungle beast annoyance. They were uneasy with his presence. The Outsider hung behind the boy, waiting for an introduction that had yet to come.

"Fucking A' man." The wild boy spoke. "We hit the liquor store on 53rd. Fuckin' old Mr. Chang, or Lee, or whatever the hell, got his melon popped. We hit Felix too. Fucking dusted him dude— that fat fuck is lying headless in his mother-fuckin' alley." The boy was a speedball of words—hot verbal smoke filled the room.

One of the larger males rose from his place on the sofa. He acknowledged not the Outsider. To the boy he gave a yes-yes head nod, and as he did so, he extended a hairy muscled arm—palm up, for payment.

"Let's get it." Slow, guttural, a voice well suited for whispered torture threats.

"Get what?"

"The fucking money, mother fucker. Let's get it."

"It was shit," the boy said, "nothing at all, we got some gas and…"

The room's uneasy calm exploded into an animal flash fire— sofas overturned, the still air scrambling for the safety of the walls. The large male grabbed the boy by the throat and forced him to the ground—pinning the wild boy beneath. The male was fast for his size, but the Outsider was also quick. He grabbed the beast by the hair and yanked his head savagely back—cracking the male's neck and pulling the stunned body to his knees. The boy broke loose, scuttled to a corner of the room and cowered against the wall, panting and waiting. The Outsider was almost full-sized now—the largest male there. He could feel the strength flowing into his hands. His bones hardening like quick steel on the forge. He owned this aggressive male.

The Outsider dug his middle finger into the right eye of his catch, pushing into the head—clawing at the soft gelatinous orb. The large male howled in pain.

"This is how it should be," the Outsider thought. *"Violence answered with violence."* His attack was not planned; he moved—instinct coursing through blood—no hate, no anger. The other males half-circled the pair. They were unable to get purchase behind the Outsider, and unsure of this new man, they did not attack. Teeth were flashed; yells and groans rent the air. They jumped and shook their arms at the Outsider—a strange vicious dance of come and go. The Outsider held his place—knee against the large male's spine, strong hand wrapped in hair. He pulled the beast's head back, the neck close to breaking, the eye crushed with intent; his conquest shook beneath him—sobbing.

The room forced itself into uneasy stillness. The only sound was the low heavy-air pumping of the man-beast's lungs. The boy crawled from the corner, stood, and eased his way between the Outsider and the others. He bowed slightly and held his arm out, palm down as he addressed his man. "It's okay," his voice feigning calm. "He didn't mean anything. He just wanted his cut. Let him up, huh?"

The Outsider watched the boy's mouth without aggression. He dug his finger deeper into the eye. The boy now faced the others, pleading one side to the next. "I met him downtown. He's okay—not us, but soon, eh—and good, huh, look at him, real good."

He turned back to his man. "It's okay. I'm all right, dude. You can let him loose huh?" The Outsider, calm but wary, released the man, who, now trying to be unseen, skulked to the back of the room—head down, unvoiced; he took a lesser place. The Outsider stood as erect as he could, and then he reached into his pocket and held out the gold tooth as an offering to the clan.

"See!" the Boy said. "Fuckin' Felix, man, I told you, we did Felix."

The males admired the prize. They passed it about, making simple hollows of their hands and rattle shaking the golden tooth.

"This is good man, real good," a shorter, heavyset male stroked the boy with the back of his hand. He smiled at the Outsider. "You got a name, man?"

The Outsider thought for some time—a question like this should have been an easy answer, but he was unsure of who he was now.

"Ha!" the heavy male exclaimed. "This motherfucker is *No One!*" The clan laughed—great deep rolling sounds of delight—braying animal lunacy.

"Hey, you guys. "No One", just gouged out T's eye!" He mimicked the attack. "Hey T, who took your peeper?" The large wounded male, sitting against the wall, briefly looked up and sheepishly displayed a cracked blood smile at the attention, but he remained in his place—at the back, as was now proper.

"Hey, T," one of the other males now joined in the calls. "You think No One wants to fuck your girl? You think he wants that?" The group, excited by the prospect of this, yelled and raged. T did not join in—he neither looked up nor smiled.

The short, heavyset male quick shuffled into an adjoining room and brought forth a female. She glanced quickly at the beaten T before she was roughly dragged before the Outsider. The heavyset male pushed her naked to the floor. The girl dropped to her hands and knees. The Outsider could see dark, angry bruises on her arms and legs—bruises faintly hidden by a thin layer of dirt. Her cunt was wet, more fouled than excited. She'd been used.

"Do you want that?" the heavyset male asked the Outsider. "Do you want to fuck that?" The Outsider looked the female over, but his cock had already made up its mind. He was harder than he'd been in years and rather than being put off by the dirt, and the scent of her used cunt, he wanted her.

"Here," the big man gestured to the floor. "Fuck her here."

The Outsider pulled down his pants and crouched behind the

female. His feet planted firmly on the floor—spread legged squat—

hands roughly holding her hips. The men offered grunts of approval and encouragement. The heavyset male yelled at the girl, "Back your ass up!"

She pushed back toward the Outsider—open, easy, no complaint or hesitation. She was his to do with as he would.

This wasn't love or any of the bullshit that Sheila had put him through. This was no god, no virginal missionary cunt, demanding the way a man might take a woman. This was as it should be, the body separated from the morals and attitudes of the weak. This was not abuse, rape, nor humiliation. He was a man and he would lay his seed in this woman.

The girl, feeling the strength of his worth, selfishly pushed against him and filled herself with the survival of her species. She surrendered her flesh to a man who could protect her young.

The Outsider threw hard, owning thrusts into the female and when he came, he grew.

She turned her face toward the Outsider. Her eyes rolled back into her head, her mouth hung open, her mind tranced with lust. The Outsider knew himself now, and the years of his oppression disappeared. He was no longer that powder-assed pussy, nancying about in his cheap car and life; he was as he always should have been—at his primal best—before he had been tamed.

The Outsider pushed the female beneath him and as she collapsed he sunk his teeth into her shoulder—biting through skin and muscle, touching bone. He marked her—branded his new mate, and then he lifted his face from her flesh and raged bloody mouthed around the room. He challenged the other males, but they let him reign. He tore off his jacket, shirt, and tie—naked, cum hanging from his cock, blood trickling from his mouth. He snarled at the men and then turned on the wild boy. He leapt and with teeth bared, grabbed

the young male and tore open his throat. The Outsider wanted no memory of his weaker self, no ties to his old life. He gnawed at the boy's face, and with his new mouth he tore flesh from remembrance. He tore at the boy's cock, tearing open his pants, pulling the testicles from the body and holding them aloft. The other males jumped and danced at the edges of the room, the female whimpering, terrified, curled at her new mate's feet.

"I am not your man!" the Outsider roared, screaming at the boy's genitals. "*I* am not *your* man!"

It was then that he remembered the other female—the woman, Sheila, the one to whom he'd been mated, and the weak cubs he'd spawned. They could not be allowed to live. And the male, the grocery clerk who had challenged his rule, he would be dealt with. The Outsider dropped the boys torn flesh to the floor as he swung toward the door. He would set things right.

Naked and untamed, he ran down the street on all fours.

An Honest Man

She was beautiful—long dark hair running like a night river to her waist, strong, olive-gold arms and legs. Her eyes were a sunburst fire sinking into an Arabian sea. If you were looking for a whore, you couldn't do better.

She was tired.

The last man had been rough. He took her unawares—flipped her, covered her mouth, and drove for her ass—entering deep and hard. She dislodged him with a sharp-toothed bite to his hand. He beat her into submission. It wasn't the first time. She was often punished for her will. She averaged fifteen to twenty men a night—most of them pigs, but an occasional old goat was thrown in to break the monotony of the contracted rape.

She painfully rose to her feet and staggered to a small corner washtub. She spread her legs and washed the remaining cum from between them. Sometimes she left it, and those who took her cared not. How many men had she known? She refused to count. But always, before they took her, she'd displayed the tattoo of the lantern stitched onto her stomach—its golden glow searching for an honest man in a hostile world. None of the johns had recognized it for what it was. And there were no honest or gentle hands.

She was thirteen when she first wore the lantern—the light from its colored-ink rays shimmered when she danced. Her tattoo went against what the religionists said about the body—the temple of the Gods, but then again, how many believers had defiled her, used her, and disregarded their truth for a few moments of pleasure. She washed her face and then reached between her legs and gently patted the unclean water against her bottom. There was blood on her hands.

"Kamana?" the housemother called.

"I'm coming." She said.

She draped a short silk gown over her bruised frame; her pride tucked neatly inside, and on her stomach was the hope that tonight he might come.

* * * * * * * * * * *

The first time she was taken, she was eight years old. It was

an uncle, a kindly old man whom she'd always adored. They were not related by blood, but Uncle was what he was called. One night he came to their home on the outskirts of the city. Her family honored him with a dinner—a feast of sorts. She sat near Uncle, his hand resting on her leg. He was gentle, more so than either her mother or her father. After dinner her mother informed her that she was to go with him, to live in his home. Contrary to what you might think a child would feel, Kamana was happy to leave. Her brothers had never been kind. They were foul and angry boys, who'd been taught by her father to steal and con. They hustled the streets near the city-center, robbing travelers and pulling quick-money scams. Whenever her father was home, he would look at her, not as a daughter, but as something from which the family could profit, like coins found in the street—a prize to be taken and spent. And her mother…she wasn't sure who her mother was. Yes, this woman lived here, but besides being a cook, a maid, and a whore to her father, her mother was no one. She might as well have called the chair she sat in 'mother'—at least she could climb into its lap.

Yes, she was happy to go with Uncle.

His house was, to her, a palace—a great villa that stood on a hill overlooking the city where she had lived. There were many rooms in Uncle's home, each one larger and grander than the last, and, Uncle had a bath—a large, ornately tiled tub that he filled with warm, clean water. She'd usually bathed with her mother in the river, and while she enjoyed the flow, it was cold at times, and dirty. When it was time to bathe, Uncle removed her clothes and gently placed her in the tub. The water felt good against her body, the soft waves of the currents gently caressed her. Uncle removed his things and climbed in. She had seen naked men before, but she laughed at his large hairy body.

"You're like a bear, Uncle!" she giggled. "A great big bear!"

Uncle smiled and rubbed the soap in his hands. He reached out for her arms and he cleansed her young skin. She closed her eyes and smiled. He was so much gentler than her mother, who, when bathing her, handled her roughly. This was wonderful. When Uncle finished, he stepped out and held a large white towel for her. This was not the rough wool sheets of her family. This towel was as soft as a summer field flower—as a cloud might feel. He dried her and then he put a sweet scented powder on his hands and ran them across her flesh. Uncle picked her up and carried her to his bedroom. It was a room larger than she'd ever seen. The windows, archways to the street, were open and the curtains gently swayed with the warm desert breeze. Tapestries covered the walls and in the center of the room, a great round bed. She had never been happier.

Uncle laid her on the bed, leaned over, and gently kissed her stomach. He climbed over her body, straddled her young form and continued his kissing—soft butterflies dancing across her neck and cheeks. He spread her legs and leaned down below her stomach. He kissed her again, this time wetter—more mouth than kiss. It felt strange, but pleasurable. Uncle kissed his way up her stomach and towards her face. Her smile lit his way. He held her hands outstretched and spread her legs wider than before, with his legs inside, gently, but firmly bracing them open. And then, as his kind face covered hers, she felt something hard where he'd kissed—something pushing against her lower stomach, making her uncomfortable. She wiggled against it, tried to move away, but Uncle held her firm. The hard thing pushed against her and then up into her stomach.

"You're hurting me!" she said. Uncle didn't stop.

He covered her mouth with his, forcing his tongue inside, causing her to swallow. She struggled to breathe. Tears ran from her eyes as if to get away. She tried with all her strength to leave, but when she rose and came toward him, the pain in her stomach got deeper, further, and hurt more.

"No Uncle!" She cried. "Please!"

But it was as if Uncle was sleeping. He wouldn't hear her. Between his thrusts she bit her lip, transferring the pain to her mouth, controlling the hurt. In her agony she wet herself. Uncle wrestled with her a bit more before he put his whole weight down upon her—a weight so great that it seemed as if it would crush her, and then he rested. Slowly the thing that had invaded her softened and went away. Uncle kissed her on the forehead and lay down to sleep.

She lived with Uncle until she was 10. She grew accustomed to his touch. She never saw her family, and rarely left his house. A week after her 10th birthday, Uncle went to the store and never returned. A few days later some men came and took her to the house in which she now lives. They gave her a new mother, and new uncles.

* * * * * * * * * * *

There was a doctor coming that morning. Someone from the city had complained about the condition of the house. In response, the rooms were swept; the beds were made, and fresh meats and fruits were brought in. It was not the house that she knew, but it made no difference—if things were nice, they were never nice for long.

When it was her turn to be examined, she was taken to one of the larger rooms. The doctor was there, and a woman in white. The doctor was kind; he spoke with her a while—pleasant conversation to make her feel at ease, but there was no need, she was going to do whatever he wanted. The doctor asked her to disrobe and then he turned his back to talk with the woman. Kamana took off everything and stood unashamed, her bruised and beaten body exposed. When the doctor turned back around he was flustered. "No, no, dear," he said. "Here, put this on." The woman in white helped her. Kamana stepped into a strange gown with ties in the back—a light blue, soft cotton dress with petite printed flowers sprinkled over the cloth. The doctor asked for her arm and gently pushed back the sleeve of her gown. He ran his hand tenderly over her bruises, a look of concern on his face. "How did you get these, dear?" he asked "Do they hit you?"

Kamana looked up into his eyes, preparing to give the story she was taught by the housemother, that she had fallen, was the clumsy sort, should've known better; but then, on meeting his glance she recoiled. For there, burning deep inside his eyes was a light, not unlike the glow from her lantern, but brighter, stronger, *real*. It was kindness and love, and it momentarily flickered before it was lost with a blink. She immediately reached down and attempted to lift her gown. He stopped her hands.

"No, please," he said. But then she tried again. "Are you trying to show me something?" he asked. Kamana nodded her head yes, and as he let her, she pulled up her gown. She showed the doctor the image of the lantern tattooed onto her stomach—the golden glow searching for an honest man. She looked at him with hope in her eyes.

"It's very beautiful." he said. "Is that what you wanted to show me?"

"Yes," she softly spoke, "I thought you would know."

The doctor smiled and asked why she'd chosen it.

"A man came and spoke in the square, and after he talked to the gathered crowd, he sat and told me a story of love and kindness. He said that somewhere there was an honest man, and if I searched for him, he could be found. After he left, I got the lantern inked into my flesh, so I could remember his story and maybe one day an honest man would see it, and know."

The doctor lowered her gown as he smiled at Kamana.

"We're going to check your blood," he told her. "Are you okay with that?" Kamana held out her wrist. "No," the doctor laughed slightly. "Here, sit down." He held her arm. "A slight stick, here." He touched the crook of her elbow. "It'll be quick, I promise. And then a shot—vitamins, for your health."

The woman in white drew the blood, and Kamana kept her eyes on the doctor. It was him, she knew it. He was gentle and kind. He cared for her. When the woman withdrew the needle and the small cotton-puffed bandage had been put in its place, the doctor turned to leave. Kamana reached for him, tenderly held his arm to entreat him to stay, but he removed her hand, smiled and assured her that one day he would return. Here, at last, was her success! Thousands of men, cities of foul-intentioned johns had passed through her, but now she had found him, and she knew, as his word, that he would return—and she could wait.

* * * * * * * * * * *

"Kamana?" the housemother called to her.

She was ready. She put on a short silk gown, perfumed her neck and inner thighs, then laid waiting on the bed.

The door opened and there he was, but without his doctor's coat, and without nurse or bag. He had come for her. She arose from the bed and held out her arms. He stepped inside, wrapped himself in her, and gently kissed her lips. She responded in kind, so gentle, so perfect—so honest. He removed her silk gown and she felt as if she was stepping into the gardens of heaven. He laid her down upon the bed—a bed that had been a platform of pain—a rack built to torture her most tender soul, but now, an altar of truth. He held her hands out to the side, and with his knees, he spread her legs. She knew what to do and pushed her hips toward him, accepting his love, freeing the spark in his eyes so that the fire he bore could consume her. He filled her. He let her arms go and she wrapped them around him, she squeezed and danced beneath him. It had taken a thousand men to get to this one, a thousand nights of despair to find one honest man in a world that was populated by vanity, lust, and hurt. She brought him closer than any person had ever been to her, and now she could feel his urgency—his body so near to hers. She felt him shake, release, and then go still. The room was filled by the silence of hope.

"Fuck…" he said. "I knew you'd be great."

"And I knew you were him," she said.

The doctor stood up and quickly grabbed his pants. "What?" he asked.

Kamana sat up on the bed. "An honest man," she said, "I knew you were an honest man."

"Ha!" the doctor laughed, "Yes, I guess I am, and great you were." He threw a handful of crumpled dollars at her. "Here you go, baby."

He walked out.

* * * * * * * * * * *

The city was a swarm of dirt that hung in the air—the dust so foul that it refused to lie back upon itself. It clung to the children and the beggars in the square. Kamana walked a stoic through the crowd, unfazed, while whispers of *"whore"* shadowed her steps. She was looking for him, the man who had spoken of honesty and love. He was a puppet of an unseen God, casting a message of white-light hope upon a gullible crowd. His followers, some of whom had fucked her, beaten her, and lied to her, stood together, clustered on a stage. One of them, his long white robes raised high above the filth, spoke his piece…

"And behold, I say to you—"

Kamana screamed above the crowd. "There is no God here!" she cried. "Look at me," she yanked up her dress exposing herself to the throng. "The lantern exposes your lies. He does not exist!"

The crowd erupted in screams. They clawed at her, beat her with their fists, and she let them. She took their fury and their hate;

she consecrated herself in the true kindness of these beasts and then she fell to the ground, unconscious, and trampled near to death by the crowd.

When Kamana awoke, she was lying face down in the dirt. She could taste the city filth mingled with the blood in her mouth. A dog, a mangy street cur, was tenderly ministering to her wounds with his tongue. She sat up, involuntarily wet herself, and then reached out to the cur. The dog, although a stray, did not run from her touch, it pulled near—gave itself to her. It was the only true affection Kamana had ever received.

"Why aren't we this?" she said, looking into the dog's eyes. "We talk so," she gestured to the holy men still preaching, the hems of their robes flecked by her blood. "But in all we've done, we can't show the kindness or the honor that these dogs show to each other. Even with nothing, they behave far above we who pray, who recognize a God. And what good is that anyway, to recognize something that we can't attain? Better to recognize this street," she reached down and held the dirt in her hands, "better to recognize the mud of the city, the clinging filth of our days, because this," she held the dirt aloft, "this is what we *can* subscribe to—a goal already met by our kind, this is what we can be."

She slowly rose and limped back towards the brothel, rubbing the soil of the city through her hair.

"This," she said, "this, is what we are."

Deconstructing God

Job was having a hell of a time getting the blowtorch to light. It looked easy on the directions, but Job wasn't mechanically inclined. He wasn't exactly sure how to use it either—at least not for the purpose he intended, but burnt skin after all, was burnt skin, whether or not you knew how to burn it. Now, if he could just get it lit.

The man in the chair was beginning to awaken—too soon, thought Job. He took a rag infused with incense and he covered the man's nose and mouth—a couple of deep breaths and his captive went under again. This man wasn't easy to catch—it took years actually, and it devastated Job's bank account, but he stayed true. The funny thing was, after chasing this prick all over the world—and he left a trail as wide as the Amazon—Job didn't catch him until he stopped looking and realized that he was already there.

Religious people have talked for years about "white-light" experiences, or "God flashes"—a shift in thinking, attitude, or ideas, that seemingly comes from outside, and yet inside, one's self. It's all very up-in-the-clouds crap, but when *you* get one—that brilliant thought that supposedly comes directly from the Almighty, well, it can be quite miraculous, and, in this case, a touch ironic. You see, Job used a "God thought" to kidnap God, and for once, that Big Honcho in the Sky was the instrument of His own undoing, instead of Him being the architect of so many others' pain.

Job slapped the passed-out body—a violent ringing shot that jerked the man's face hard to the right. The ground shook, reverberating from the slap to the end of existence, but Job didn't care; he had him now. He'd caught God. The blowtorch sprang to life.

* * * * * * * * * * *

It was a Monday, a workday, a pray about not losing your job day, and Job had placed himself directly in front of the tallest building of finance—a building dedicated to the "In God We Trust" eye of this Man. Where better, if God were going to be anywhere, than this building, on this day? God had always wanted to be served and adored.

Job dressed himself in the clothes of a street beggar—a modern-day leper on 2nd Street—a one-hand-out pain in the ass creeping desperately along the boulevard, loser. God could never resist a beggar; especially if it looked like that beggar's skin was in danger of falling off. Job was a cunning man. He wasn't always so, but circumstances had forced him to evolve. The day before, Job had stopped by a butcher's shop and bought a bucket of lamb's blood—fresh, un-coagulated Little Bo-Peep purity—and this morning, Job had bathed in it.

A rag, tucked neatly in Job's pocket, was infused with dust of frankincense and myrrh.

Job was ready, but this wasn't going to be easy. The Almighty wouldn't appear bearded and robed, voice thundering throughout the city. God was a tricky fuck; he could be anyone. But Job had a feeling that it would be something in the eyes and the general behavior of the man—something beyond worldly, that would give God away. Job sat at the curb for hours before God arrived. And when He did come, He was in the guise of a stock trader—a briefcase slinging gunfighter of commerce.

God approached Job. He took a deep breath. It was the lamb's blood—chum on the skin of man, which lured the Great Holy Shark of the Universe. The stock trader opened his wallet.

"Here you go buddy," the man who just might be God said, as he handed Job a five-dollar bill. "A little something to make it easier. You have a good day now, okay?"

Oh, wasn't he the benevolent one, thought Job.

The stock trader had a kind face, but it was not soft—a strong jaw and a male-model nose gave he who might be God a handsome poster boy visage. His light brown hair with a touch of distinguished grey at the temples framed God's good looks. Job looked into his eyes; or rather, he looked through his eyes and was sucked into a telescope of light as deep as the cosmos. Thank this man before him that Job had covered himself with blood, or he would've most surely been caught, and his unrighteous intentions displayed before the most Holy Lord God of Hosts. God was thankfully distracted by the scent of innocence and Job's intent of malice went unseen.

"Thank you, sir." Job was quick with the pleasantries. "But it is going to be a great day."

"And why's that, son?" asked He who was now most assuredly God.

"Because, I'm going to see something that I've never seen before, something even greater than *this*." Job reverently held up the five-dollar bill. The man before him, or rather his eyes, the same as the one drawn over the great pyramid, looked at the money with a touch of self-absorbed interest.

"And what could that possibly be?" God asked.

"I'm going to see a sacrifice," Job said, "a real burnt offering."

The man who was God lit as if he was privy to an inside line on an under-the-table trade. "Really," he asked, "and can…uh, just anyone, see this…uh…offering?"

Job hooked him, but now he needed to reel him in. There was a van waiting at the rear of the building, tucked into the loading dock.

"I don't know," Job carefully displayed his thoughts. "I guess so. Hell, why not? I've got a vehicle parked out back…that is, if you'd like to come?" God looked Job over, judging him on his not-exactly-homeless ruse.

"I know," Job said, gesturing to his circumstance, "it ain't really honest, but a guy has to make a living, right?"

The man, the one called God, smiled. "Yeah, I guess you're right. Now let's go take a peek at that offering."

They walked toward the rear of the building, God on occasion, deeply inhaling, filling himself with the scent of the blood beneath

Job's clothes. It was like a plateful of hot cookies to a hungry child, a room chock-full of grandma's house aroma—and Job led this living, most dangerous Creator, to the loading dock.

The van was rented. It was a cargo type, black with tinted windows. If you were of the paranoid sort, you might think it a vehicle to transport agents of the government, but it wasn't. Job had picked it up from Harold's on W. 30th, a cut-rate rental place that wasn't too particular when it came to the moral or dirty-business leanings of their clientele.

"The door can be a bit sticky," Job said. "Here, let me get that." He opened and held the door for God. "You get what you pay for, huh?"

God began to climb in, but Job, quick as an angel, had other ideas. He pulled the incense-infused rag from his pocket and with it he covered God's nose and mouth. The deity dropped like a swarm of drunken locusts on Egypt. Job, a roll of grey duct tape now in hand, secured the rag to God's face. He dragged the passed out deity to the rear of the van and loaded Him inside. His Most Holy Personage was now luggage.

It was a ballsy move, this God trap that Job had sprung; would the lamb's blood lull God into a satiated state of docileness?

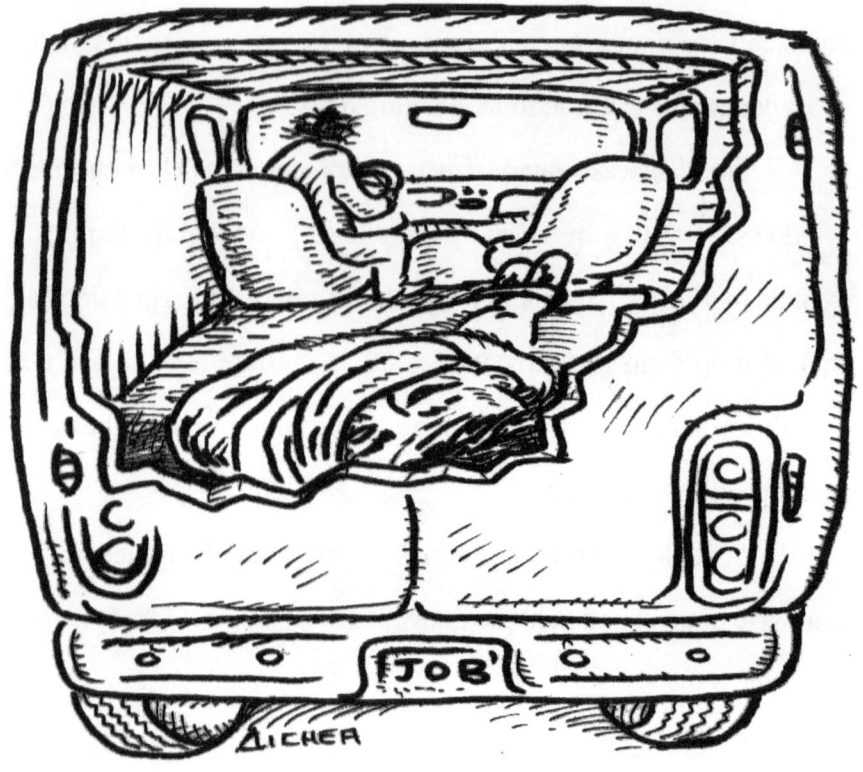

Would the frankincense and myrrh really knock him out? Job wasn't sure, and he was risking an eternity in Hell on his guesses. But Job was very angry at the passed out Creator lying in the cargo area of his van. So, whether it worked or not, he'd been willing to try. What was that old Bible line, *"...if you have faith and do not doubt, not only can you do what was done to the fig tree, but also you can say to this mountain, 'Go, throw yourself into the sea,' and it will be done."* Job had faith.

God was the bane of man—the death, the destruction, the wars, and the natural disasters that have shaken this world since its creation, they'd all originated from Him, this duct-taped, cargo-riding fuck.   And Job had also tasted a bit of God's handiwork himself, and it was that taste that brought him to this place.

Job drove the van to a block of old warehouses near the docks. He was neither stopped nor hindered along his way—with God out of the picture, things were running quite smoothly in the world. He pulled in front of one of the smaller buildings, hopped out, and rolled up the big double door. He drove the van in and pulled the door down behind him. Job had prepared his place; lamb's blood was sprinkled on the floor, and the sweet, spicy, smoke of incense rose from large black cauldrons. Smoke to keep God sedated and unable to reach into his bag of Godly tricks. *Job was gonna let him have it.* God would soon be held accountable for his crimes against humanity. The Heavenly Cargo was dragged from the van and rough-rope tied to a chair—*now, where was that fucking torch?*

* * * * * * * * * * *

Job ran the flame across the sleeping God's face—a Haley's Comet trail of burnt flesh appeared.

"Wakey, wakey, Mr. God. It's time to meet your

Makey." Job had been desperately waiting for this moment and he was a bit giddy—borderline manic actually.

"WAKE UP, MOTHERFUCKER!" Job screamed as he punched God in the balls.

God woke. "What are you doing? Where am I? *What are you doing?*"

"You don't know?" Job was happier than he'd been in years. "The Big Mapmaker in the Sky doesn't know where he is? I thought you created *all* this?" Job twirled about the room like a demented Julie Andrews. "We're in that piece of shit warehouse that you built on the waterfront—the one near your homeless camp, off 24th Street."

"What are you talking about? I didn't build anything. What are you doing?"

"I'm getting ready for an offering—one that you wanted to see, a big chunk of your Holy flesh in exchange for all the innocents you've killed."

"I didn't kill anybody. I'm a stock trader for fuck sake. Let me go!"

The air was thick with incense—not enough to put God under, but a heavenly cloud of local anesthesia. Job walked over to a table and picked up a pair of bolt cutters. He waved them at God. "You can cut locks with these," Job said as he rolled up a desk chair and sat before his Creator—burning-bush close.

"You ever see someone lose a finger or a hand?" Job asked. "Oh, wait, what am I saying, of course you have. You've seen lots of that, yeah? It's a shame, because you did such a beautiful job making these." Job reached out and stroked God's hand. God tried to pull away but his arms were anchored to the chair, his wrists securely tied. Job caressed God's ring finger with the sharp edged tip of the cutters.

"Stop it! I don't know you. I didn't do anything! I'm not who you think I am."

"YOU DIDN'T DO ANYTHING?" Job stood and leaned over God. "You're not who I think you are? I know who you are motherfucker, and I have a beginning-of-the-world list of your crimes. How many FUCKING people have you killed?"

Job chopped off the ring finger of God—the bone breaking as a weak winter branch—and as the finger fell it disintegrated in mid air—a clean cut and break—no blood.

"Well, look at that," Job said. "Disappearing fingers, and no blood. And you said I didn't know who you were. Well, fuck you.

I know you." Job bent down and whispered to God. "Does it hurt? Can you feel pain?"

God gave Job the look of one resigned to his fate, but still, there was anger there—a stern hurricane stare that tore through the smoke-filled room like black lightning in a snowstorm. The world shook, and the coasts of Africa became none.

"I don't care if you can feel it," Job said, "because I can. I can feel good about this, and about what I'm going to do to you. I'm gonna take you down one pride-filled piece at a time—so many crimes you'll pay for, so many lives." Job reached down, pulled up his trousers, and grabbed a large knife that he'd strapped to his leg. He flashed it through the air, and sliced God's face, not once, but many times, each cut punctuated with a word—

"One."

"Fucking."

"Piece."

"Atta."

"Time."

Job stopped slicing and snatched a roll of parchment from the table. It was a large roll, 10 or 12 inches across—and he displayed it before the Almighty. Written across the top, in a hand steady and true, the words: "Crimes Committed Against the World by His Most Unholy Lord – actual name and address unknown."

Job read the first charge.

"The person known as God influenced the killing of two innocent lambs in order to clothe a creation, Man, which he hath made. They were brutally murdered."

"Ha!" Job said. "The first in what looks to be a very long day of atonement. Innocent lambs—animal abuse is a crime worthy of at least this." Job took the torch to God's right ear—the skin of which melted in the flame like a wax candy treat. God did not scream.

The continent of Asia was no more.

Job worked well into the evening. He slashed and burned his way into the 21st century. The list of crimes levied against God was horrible and frightening, and Job carried out his punishments with zeal. Job spoke for those who could not. He struck back for those who had been hit, and he burned flesh for the holocaust of the ages. God, tied to the chair, was less now than He had been. His toes and fingers gone, His clothes burnt from His body, His flesh seared to bone, but He was still conscious, and the world had become an island of this room, and these two—Job and God.

The scroll had been unfurled—a mile of parchment lying brown paper spent, covering the floor of the room, in large, damning piles.

"And now it's my turn," Job said. He reached into his breast pocket and pulled out a small photo of a woman—a brunette with love-touched eyes and lips. The photo was well worn.

"Do you remember her?" Job asked. "Do you remember this

one?"

Job grabbed the back of God's head. His fingers sunk into the now putrid flesh. He pulled Him close and held the photo before what used to be God's eyes.

"Do you remember her?" Job said. "This was my wife, and you took her."

God shook his head no.

"Don't fucking 'NO' me!" Job screamed. "Look at her!" He shoved the photo into God's face. "She was an angel! A fucking angel and she never hurt anyone. You had no right to take her. You had no fucking right!"

With all he had left, Job slapped God—spit slow motion flew from the deity's mouth.

"What had she done to you, to anyone?" Job said. "She didn't deserve to die."

God was silent.

"Say something!" Job screamed. He gestured to a world that was no longer there. He waved at the emptiness of retribution. "You did this! You fucking caused this!"

God whispered low on his breath, the words falling from his mouth as a beaten dove falls from the sky.

"What did you say?" Job imitated his whisper—intense, listening for some remorse. "What did you just say?"

God's eyes were gone, His nose broken, His teeth swallowed into the stomach of His pain.

"Speak!" Job ordered. "Say something!"

"You can't do this," God said. "You can't kill Me, Job."

"But I can do it," Job said, "and I will. I made you pay for what you've done. I'm holding you accountable."

God looked in the direction of his accuser—he was incapable of seeing him, but he knew where he was.

"You can't kill me Job, because this is *my* dream. I dreamed you, and the heavens, and the earth, I created all this as I slept. *You* can't kill *me*."

The still of an eternal night wrapped itself around what was left of the universe. Job, almost satisfied, smiled. "But I can," he said. "I can kill you. I have faith, and it's your promise. I can move a mountain to the sea if I believe and I do. I have faith, and for her, I will."

Job plunged the knife into the heart of God.

The lights went out in the world.

The Crosstown Bulls: A Love Story

Richard cowered behind the waist-high, chain-link fence. He was in danger of getting beaten, possibly stomped to death, by the large bull dyke, Margaret and her companion, Ida. The ladies were a pair of what the sensitive men in the neighborhood called "Battle-Dykes"—a gang of large, cruising, female thugs who would like nothing more than to have a bit of brutal sport with a gentle man like Richard. He was a "Miss Nancy Boy", or Nancy for short. The Nancies were a gang of sorts—more of a protection society really, who figured they'd better band together before they were individually torn apart. Richard closed his eyes and held his breath. He hoped for safe passage. No such luck.

"Well, look-it here…" One of the dykes grabbed Richard by the neck and hoisted him over the fence like a plucked flower. She shook the dirt from his stem.

"What you got, Margaret?" Her companion jumped in—and on.

"Looks like I got me a little 'ass-cleaner' with a real pretty mouth." She made Richard pucker by squeezing his cheeks—hard. "What do you say, 'little lady'?"

"I'm a man, dammit. You let me go!" Richard hung from her hand, kicking and squirming in the air.

"Now, why would I do that?" Margaret asked. "I'm feeling all gushy-wushy back here," she rubbed her large ass with her free hand, "and I need tending to."

"Why don't we take him 'round back?" Ida said. "I could use a 'lil sprucing up myself."

The big bulls laughed as they dragged Richard behind the building.

"Come on Ida, pull his things off."

Margaret held Richard around the chest as Ida pulled off his shoes and pants. Her large hands were not gentle. She tore his finery, destroyed his silk shirt. Richard wore a pair of light blue bikini briefs beneath his trousers. This undergarment brought the two bulls no small measure of enjoyment…until his briefs were removed and his extremely small penis was exposed.

"Well, fucking look at that!" Ida was pointing and laughing. She grabbed one of Richard's legs and held it high in the air— "spread-eagling" the poor, naked man. She took a finger and put it aside his cock—her little finger, his even littler prick. She squealed with laughter. "Your buddies must have thimble asses!"

Margaret threw Richard to the ground and flipped him onto his back. Ida held him as Margaret dropped her very large, very dirty trousers and exposed her equally large and extremely dirty bottom. She sat squarely down on Richard's face, burying his head between her overly ample bare ass-cheeks.

"Clean it up, bitch!" She wriggled, sinking lower.

Richard kicked his feet. He was in danger of suffocating— beginning to feel lightheaded—when Margaret shifted forward and let him catch a whiff of stale, sour air. He gasped—then retched.

"You either start licking little lady," she hissed, "or I take you out."

Richard knew that if he didn't follow orders, she might kill him, and being suffocated by a large, unclean woman's ass was not his way to go. He stuck out his tongue and touched it against her cheek. She shifted up again.

"You're going to get hurt bitch, if you don't get in that hole right now. Stop fucking around and clean it!" Margaret took her hands and spread her ass cheeks wide, exposing her anus. "Lick it!"

Richard put his tongue against Margaret's hole and licked. It tasted both sharp and sour—rotten flesh fruit, but like a good boy he did his job—licking and cleaning the large woman's behind. And the more he licked, the taste abated, so like a dog, he hungrily lapped at her ass.

"That's it baby, lick it up," Margaret's deep gravely voice cooed.

"Hey, we gotta good one here," Ida moaned and rubbed her fat crotch. "We should take him back and…oh fuck!" Ida pointed toward Richard's genitals. "Look at that! Look at his little dick!"

Richard was erect.

"Oh my God, Margaret. Your 'lil ass cleaner's dick is hard. Look out! He's gonna put your fucking eye out with that thing." The Bulls mocked and roared with laughter.

Across the street, a small gang of Nancy Boys was getting up their nerve—an intervention steeled by their feminine protective nature. They huddled together like a bevy of 15-year-old schoolgirls and smooth-hustled their way across the street.

"Leave him alone!" one of the Nancys yelled. It was Tommy,

a real keen dancer from Temple City. He picked up a small, broken tree branch and led the charge.

The Bulls gazed up toward the boys like a pair of lions interrupted during a tender meal of gazelle. They were irritated by the soft invasion of their mealtime. The Cuban heel-clicking advance of the Nancys worried them not. Undeterred, they turned back to their sport. There was another ass to clean. Ida wanted her turn.

The Nancy Boys closed in. Tommy whacked Ida in the back with his branch. His palms stung from the force of the blow. She lifted her fat ass from Richard's face and shook Tommy like an extremely well put-together rag doll. A simple gold bracelet fell from his wrist, and his pocketbook skittered off under a bush.

"Eeeeeeeeeeeee!"

Tommy exhaled a high-pitched scream that, instead of frightening the other Nancys, inflamed the gang. They swarmed the big bulls—six Nancys on two Battle Dykes—scratching and biting and slapping the girls, but their attack was futile. The Dykes were too much for the boys. During the skirmish Richard broke free, clambered to his feet and tried to run, but Margaret quickly retrieved him. She tucked him under her arm, and jogged toward the street. Ida followed.

The Battle Dykes could have easily beaten these boys if that was their whim, but a large commotion meant police presence, so they hurried their way down the block. The Boys gave chase, but to the Bulls, they were no more dangerous than an expensively perfumed cloud of agitated dust. The big dykes turned the corner and ran down the alley with their prey dangling beneath Margaret's large arm like a scuffed-up kid leather handbag.

* * * * * * * * * * *

The bulls carried Richard to a clubhouse bar on the far side of town. He'd been there before. Sometimes the Nancies, after getting liquored up, would drive by and yell curses at the windows—a few light pink cosmopolitans coaxed brave threats from the boys. The bar had that sour malt odor, and Richard wasn't sure if it was the spilt beer on the floor or a contagion of yeast infections. He grimaced and thought of the thick taste of Margaret's behind.

The bar was packed with Battle Dykes—catcalls and laughter danced drunkenly around Richard as he was pawed and groped. They forced him into a leather harness—a gay gladiator's suit with loops and studs. Richard's frail body struggled to fill it out, and it sagged unfashionably upon him. He was led on a chain to a dark corner of the bar and forced to kneel on worn red carpet.

He was secured; legs and arms behind him, head tied with a leather
cord and pulled forcefully back. The Dykes handcuffed Richard to a
metal bar. If Richard hadn't recently completed the Linda Fairchild
Yoga Series it would have surely broken his neck.

From Richard's now very limited viewpoint, he could
see Margaret at the bar. She was writing—a thick black pen on

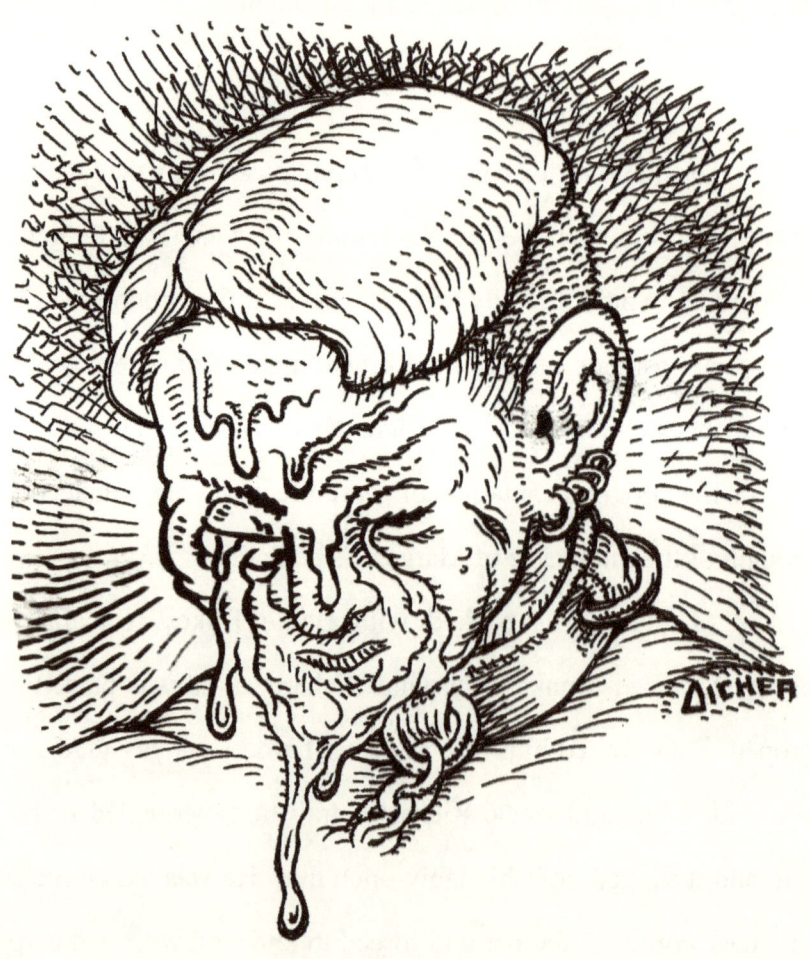

cardboard. It looked to be a sign of some sort. She finished and stood before Richard, holding the cardboard out for his perusal—it read: TOILET. She took a metal coat hanger, stretched it wide, and placed it around his neck. She hung the sign from it. Richard was mortified. This was worse than he thought. The bulls lined up, one after the other, taking turns discharging previously digested beer onto Richard's face. He gagged and sputtered on the urine. A few of the dyke's streams were so hard and long that Richard was forced to inhale, choke and unfortunately, swallow some of their waste. Thankfully, his tears didn't show on his piss-soaked face. Surely, Richard thought, the Nancy Boys would come to his aid, but after many hours of Merle Haggard on the jukebox, he knew he would not be saved.

* * * * * * * * * * *

On the other side of town, unbeknownst to Richard, the Nancy Boys had stitched together a brave plan. They would procure ballet slippers, preferably unworn, and the majority a nice size seven men's. Then they would don black garb—not leather mind you, more of a form-fitting, dark grey, chiffon, and they would soft shoe their way into the bar and sneak Richard out after everyone had left.

* * * * * * * * * * *

It'd been a long night. Richard's neck was sore and cramped. His throat burned from the urine and the acid of regurgitation, his stomach distended, filled with the piss of fifty beer-quaffing Bulls. He was a mess.

The bar was almost empty now save for a few voices. Richard couldn't see who they belonged to, but one of them was most definitely Margaret's. She was giving instructions to someone—someone with a gentler, more feminine sound—but not a man.

"You get that bitch hosed down and clean this place up," Margaret ordered. "Rodrigo will get the glasses in the morning, but I want that fucking floor swept and the bar wiped down. Ida and I are going up to bed, so you keep yourself and *her* quiet. When you're done, secure that little pisspot in the back room and find something to cover her. We don't want our toilet to get cold and go dying on us…" A deep evil laugh punctuated the order. Richard heard heavy retreating footsteps and a door slam. He was alone with the gentle voiced girl.

Richard could hear movement and a faucet being turned on, and then…he was hit with a cold hard stream of water. *He* was the "bitch" getting hosed down. The water stung but Richard leaned into it as he caught the fresh-air scent that it brought. He gagged, threw up a quart of piss, and then inhaled deeply of the clean, cold stream.

A face appeared over Richard. She looked young and not unkind—mid-20s, brunette, with easy doe brown eyes. *What was she doing hanging with this crowd?* Richard envied her fresh, clean skin.

"God, look what they've done to you." The girl pushed Richard's wet bangs away from his eyes. At first, he recoiled from her touch, but now he craved her soft hand. "You're a mess, baby." Richard started to sob as she unlocked the shackles on his feet. She removed the chain.

"You better not run now."

Richard shook his head 'no'. He was scared and he hadn't the strength to run. When she loosed the tie holding his head, Richard stretched and blushed—he was embarrassed, humiliated over the abuse that he'd taken. The girl walked to the bar, grabbed a clean towel, and wrapped it around Richard. She gently patted and rubbed him dry.

"Can I ask you something?" Richard's voice was weak, shaky, and apologetic.

"Sure. What do you want to know?"

"You're not like them. Why are you here?" asked Richard. "Why are you being so kind to me?"

The girl laughed. "I am like them, kind of, but I guess I'm just here for protection, really."

Richard nodded his head—*ah, a kindred soul*.

"That's why I joined the Nancy Boys. I'm not really like them either, but I'm small. I get picked on a lot, and women usually frightened me. I don't hate girls; actually, I like the way they look— not Margaret or Ida, but girls like…you. What's your name?"

"They call me Bunny," the girl replied, "Little Bunny."

"That's nice," Richard said. "Really nice."

* * * * * * * * * *

Outside, the Nancy Boys were ready to make their move. They'd arrived in three cars—a long black Cadillac limousine and two olive-green Subaru wagons with sport roof racks—the Boys rightfully thought that Richard was probably upset and a touch of luxury might ease his pain. They carried baseball bats—not heavy hitters, but little Louisville Sluggers, and they meant business. From the bushes across the street they'd watched the bar empty of its patrons, and now, it was their turn to move. Silent and cat-like, they tiptoed toward the door.

* * * * * * * * * * *

Richard sat next to Bunny—she gently rubbed his shoulders, caressed his sore neck. He smiled into her eyes. Richard followed the urge to lean forward and kiss the first girl of his life—a kiss that was not refused, but accepted and returned with vigor. She was smaller than the other girls, but still larger than Richard. She held his head in her hands and guided his lips around hers. It was not unpleasant, and Richard was not afraid.

* * * * * * * * * * *

The Nancy Boys marched—wickedly out of formation, twirling their small bats as they quietly opened the door and sashayed inside. They advanced on the kissing pair. Bunny was on top of Richard, tenderly holding him down. Richard, in ecstasy, let himself be devoured by her lips. He opened his eyes for only a second to see if the kiss was really true, when a boldly tasseled, chiffon-black arm swung through the air and a junior Louisville Slugger slammed into the right side of Bunny's face. The Boys swarmed about her like a sadistic flock of hummingbirds.

"NOOOO!" Richard screamed. "NOT HER! NOOOO!"

But it was too late, the rage of fifteen tiny cocks exploded in

Bunny's direction. She was beaten, savagely. Richard struggled to help her, but he was quick-hustled out the door and whisked toward the waiting cars. The Boys were merciless with Bunny, well, as merciless as they were capable of, which meant a few hard swings and then a hasty retreat—their soft slippers making no sound on the beer and yeast-soaked floor.

Richard was wrapped in a light cream-colored robe of soft terrycloth and tucked into the backseat of the long black sedan. Against his protestations, he was comforted by members of his gang—one boy on each side—stroking and fawning over the trembling man. The other Nancies hopped into the waiting cars— the mission accomplished.

Ida and Margaret burst from the door. They were furious, fists clenched, shaking great sleepy arms in the air. Richard couldn't hear their curses but he could feel their heat. Bunny followed limping from the club—a bloody, wet rag held to her face. She reached a hand toward the car, grasping for Richard. The Nancy, protected by his gang, wistfully peered through the back window of the sedan, his heart fiercely beating.

They drove away.

* * * * * * * * * * *

The Boys brought Richard to a neat penthouse apartment on the corner of Broadway and 7th. They bathed him and washed away the outer disgrace of his torment. They did not pry. The Boys compassionately waited for Richard to speak.

"It was horrible," he said. "They beat me and they used me… but there was one, one girl, the one I kissed that was different. She was kind and gentle, loving and sweet—"

"And she was young," Tommy broke in, "and she was dangerous and got what she deserved."

"No," Richard argued, "she was different. She wasn't like them."

"Richard, you were hurt and confused. People do strange things under stress. I once dated a girl."

"You did?" The attending Nancy Boys asked in unison.

"Yes," Tommy continued, "and she was like your girl. She was sweet and kind at first, we even slept together, once. But she got older, and wider, and less put together, and then one day she changed, just like yours would. It's her nature Richard, and as sweet as you thought she was, you can't go against nature. Let it go, stay here where you're loved and protected—where you belong." Tommy stroked Richard's hair and then gently squeezed his neck.

"There's a great new DJ at the hotel, and after a few cosmos, you'll forget all about those nasty old things and this terrible day."

Richard leaned against Tommy and smiled. The silk pant leg of Tommy's slacks felt cool and comforting against Richard's face.

"You're right Tommy, I *was* confused and this is where I belong, with you, and the boys.

Richard stretched his neck and soaked in the loving protection of the gang. He stood and the smart cut of his pajamas hung squarely off his shoulders—a beautiful Japanese silk.

"I am feeling better," he said, "and maybe tonight, after a couple of cocktails, we could drive by that clubhouse and catch one of those bulls—give her a taste of what they gave me, a little retribution for their nasty ways."

"That's the spirit!" the boys cheered.

"It's too bad though," Richard said.

"What's too bad, Richard?"

"It's too bad we're not beer drinkers."

"Ohhh," the Boys exclaimed in disgust. "Why?"

Richard reached out and lustfully stroked Tommy's cock through his slacks.

"Because, I bet those cosmopolitans taste just as nice second hand."

Arthur Chance Punk Rock Detective

The broken glass flashed hazardous starlight in his eyes as he combed the alley. *"It was here,"* he thought, *"this is where they snatched her."*

He was a private detective—a punk rock purveyor of the cases the police couldn't or wouldn't touch. Arthur Chance was a 'dick,' and at times his methods matched his title. Too many kicks in the head and a nose for cheap inhalants had made him less than stable, but he got the job done, and his body recovery rate was practically perfect.

He bent down, dipped a finger in the foul alley goo, and popped it in his mouth. He could taste the blood—and the urine. The girl had been assaulted and went missing two nights ago. He'd heard it was a real public trip—a catfight that turned into a beating, which morphed into some sort of a gangbang, ending in a missing persons case. If he wasn't on the job, it sounded like his sort of fun. And, he wasn't surprised that the girl's family had been a little slow to pull the trigger on his services; straights were always a bit wary of cats like him—*scared fucks, they'd probably thought the police would save their baby—too bad their tax dollars were being spent on glazed donuts and dick hardeners. The boys in blue weren't too concerned about a missing punkette—probably figured she was a runaway who got tired of being yelled at for sucking dick and replacing dad's booze with water. It would be weeks before the pigs took it serious—if ever. Her parents were wise to call him.*

"Fuckin' A," he thought, "a little bitch like that; she's gonna get passed around like a cheap drink." He took another look at her picture and smiled—she was less than attractive, "Oh well, maybe they're not fucking her, but they ain't being sweet."

There was a club on the corner, an all-ages joint where he could swing in for a drink and a slam. He didn't care who was playing, he just needed some hard fast music and a roll through the pit—and if a wild elbow got thrown, so be it, he loved bustin' heads and a little violence was all part of the show.

The bartender was an old, one-eyed hippie, with a speech impediment. He knew him—a real slow-talking knob with a stingy pouring hand and a ten-ninety haircut. Arthur called out for a cold beer.

"Let's get a Pabst, Ames." The hippie grabbed a brew from the top of the ice-chest. "Nah, man," Arthur said. "Get your fuckin' arm down there and grab me a cold one. You think I'm some fuck?"

"Nuh, no, Arthur," the hippie replied. "You…you're not a fuck."

He would've whacked the big dummy in the puss for being a cunt, but he felt sorry for the poor bastard. Motherfucker probably thought Nixon was still running the show. He laid his leather jacket across the bar and took a long pull off his beer.

"You seen Greasy Steve?" Arthur said. "I heard he was hanging around here."

Greasy Steve was the local porn king—sweeping up young punk girls from the suburbs and turning them into inner-city cum-rags. Arthur wasn't positive Greasy was involved, but this sounded like his thing; violence and bitch snatching was right up his line.

"Yeah," Ames said, "he was over here a few nights ago, hanging with the midget Paul, and that chick from Duarte."

"The Mexican chick; the one with the tattoo of Jesus on her ass?"

"I don't know nothing about a tattoo, Arthur, but if you're talking about that girl with the big hair, yeah, that's her."

Arthur knew her. The chick was dirty and mean—rolled arrogant with a beehive hairdo ratted with razor blades inside, but she was a good fuck—you had to go double-condom thick when you were hitting it, but all in all, it was good. He took a wild stab.

"I heard she got in a fight last week, boxing some fat bitch in the alley."

The big hippie lit up. "Yeah, that was it. I saw 'em arguing near the toilets and then they started pushing and squawking—some blonde chick and her, a real aggressive trip, man."

"Was Steve in on it?"

"I don't know, man. It looked like…yeah, maybe…fuck, I don't know. I just stay out of it man." The big hippie wandered over to serve another beer. Arthur downed his, grabbed his jacket and headed for the door.

It didn't take a genius to solve these cases; evil usually operates in its own backyard. Most of these fucking dirt-bags are too lazy to pull jobs across town, so they shit in their own pool. You got a burglary, you cruise 14th looking for junkies and tweakers. You got a bitch grab; you dive into the warehouse sewers where you got your deviants and your sex-for-money film cats. Fucking cops— wandering around like Sherlock-fucking-Holmes when all they do is cruise the shopping market of trash and pick perpetrators off the aisles—I could've been a cop. I look great in blue.

Greasy Steve lived over on 81st near the water. Arthur knew the place; he'd done some stunt-cock work on a couple of Steve's films—if you're hard up for cash, having a dick without stage fright and a I-don't-give-a-fuck-who-sees-this attitude can net you some bills. Arthur climbed up the fire escape. The apartment was on the third floor. It was an easy climb and an even easier time finding Greasy's pad—the windows were covered with aluminum foil—"fucking tweaking fuck". Most of these porn cats were tweakers—stay up all week, fuck, and make movies. He put his head against the window and listened for noise. It was quiet, and quiet meant nobody home. If those freaks were in there they'd be building shit and jabbering about descendants of lizard people and who knows what. He knew it was cool. He kicked in the glass and climbed inside. Instantly he was hit with the scent of chemicals and fuck stink. "Jesus, they've been at it hard in here."

There was a big naked girl tied to the chair. The rope was buried deep in her marbled flesh. She was hooded and her head hung down on her chest. If her skin weren't still pink he would've thought she was dead. He walked over and slapped her. Her head jerked up and she started mumbling.

"Mmmphhh mphhh, mphhh." Arthur laughed. He undid the hood and pulled it off. It was she. The girl he was looking for.

"You having fun, baby?" Arthur said.

"Mmmphhh mphhhhhh." He pulled the duct tape off her mouth and she spit out a dirty sock.

"He's in the fucking toilet!" she said.

Arthur turned as the midget Paul walked into the room. He was naked; holding a knife, and his limp cock hung to his knees. Arthur smiled at the girl in the chair, "You been hitting that?"

"Get the fuck outta here, Arthur." The midget advanced with the blade. "I'll fucking cut you, man."

"Yeah, about that," Arthur said. He reached into his jacket pocket and slid on a pair of brass knuckles. "You better get carving, gimp."

The little man ran at Arthur, knife slashing wildly, but Arthur was quick, he sidestepped the dwarf, and cracked him in the back of the head with the brass. The midget dropped face first to the floor; his cock lying like a long black tail between his bowed legs. Arthur untied the girl. She stood shivering near his side. He picked up the knife and nodded at the midget's cock.

"You want me to cut that dick off so you can take it home?" She said nothing. Arthur picked up a blanket that was lying nearby and tossed it at her. She wrapped herself in it and sat down.

"Where's Greasy Steve and the bitch?" Arthur said.

"They went out to get Chinese and I'm fucking starving."

"Well, we could hang out here and wait till they get back, but they ain't gonna be too happy about old Paul, and the fact that your naked ass is no longer strapped to that chair is gonna be a big cause for concern." He moved beside her and with the back of his hand roughly caressed her cheek. She didn't resist. "What were they doing to you, anyway? Why'd they grab ya?"

"They took my fucking boots," she said, "and my leather." She stood and walked over to the midget. "And they were filming as this thing fucked me." She stomped her big bare foot down on the dwarf's dick—he remained still, unconscious. "I don't know what the fuck they wanted."

She was lying. This bitch was too cool and too easy to

not be mixed up with something. Fuck it, he didn't care, he was looking forward to some dough and a blowjob on the way back to her parents.

"Let's roll baby." He walked to the door.

The girl followed.

~ to be continued…

Once Was an Angel

He'd been summoned a million times—humans, at the point of some hurt or edge of death terror, reaching out for help from beyond their world—and he'd responded. It was the duty of his kind to walk these streets, serve these beasts, these mutant children of God—and Darius, the Angel, had grown to resent it.

"Why should I serve them?" he thought. *"Why should my life be spent doting like a cur at the heels of these men? I'm equal to God in their world, and yet, I'm no better than a slave."*

On this fall afternoon, Darius had been summoned to the Seaside rest home, "Near the ocean, by the shore."

"Yes," he giggled, *"the shore marking the end of your pathetic little lives."*

Darius was tall; his skin a deathly blue-marble white and from his back rose great magnificent wings that when unfurled spanned the length of two men. His tail swung great serpentine strides behind him. There was a wheelchair blocking his way, so a slight shove he gave—the chair's elderly occupant startled by the unseen force that rocketed his senility down the hall and into an orderly's tray—which was stacked with the 4pm easy-to-digest meals.

"This place reeks of death," Darius said.

He dipped a long crooked finger into a vanilla pudding cup and then wriggled his nose in disgust.

"Is this your idea of a joke," he said, as he glanced toward the heavens, "artificial manna, for the nearly deceased?"

Darius strolled into the room of an old woman and sat down on a chair near her bed. She was about to swallow a pill that would become lodged in her throat. Without Darius' intervention, she would die.

"What's the point?" he thought. *"Here she is, lying in her own filth—a burden to her family, and of service to no one. She's a tax upon those around her, and yet…"* He again looked above, *"You want her around for what, another three or four days of worshipping You?"*

Darius leaned back in the chair and put his size seventeen feet on her bed. He was wearing shiny black leather boots that went remarkably well with his red, sharkskin suit.

"I think I'll let her die—watch her choke on the antidote of her ills."

He folded his arms and waited in patient repose.

The old woman, with skeletal hands, put the large white pill in her mouth and Darius watched with glee as her ancient old puss opened wide and then chomped down on her supposed savior. She began to gasp—a wrinkled old fish flopping about on a yellowed Sear's Posturepedic mattress—fighting for breath. Darius was unmoved. He enjoyed her suffering, but then, instinctively, he was forced to act. He materialized in front of the old woman, grabbed her head, and snaked his long tongue deep within her mouth. It crawled into the back of her throat where it roped the pill and brought it forth, saving her life. She exhaled a large dry dusty cloud of stale old woman breath—Darius retched. He shoved the old woman down on the bed and jumped on top of her—sitting on her hips, riding her like a flipped over nag. He roughly grabbed her ears and pulled her pruney face close to his—her old bones painfully popped and cracked.

"Do you know where you are, mother?" he hissed at her. *"Do you enjoy this?"*

He released his tongue and took a long wet swipe up her face. The old woman froze to the sheets in static shock—this monster, carnally real.

"What are you?" she croaked.

Darius lifted into the air above her and smiled as wide as heaven's host.

"I'm your savior," he said.

And he vanished from the room.

* * * * * * * * * * *

"I'm telling you Zeke, I can't take it any more. I think I'm losing it. I'm turning into a real vicious prick. And what's the point anyway, I mean…really, you've been doing this as long as I have—do you ever wonder why?"

Ezekiel took a quick glance around the office.

"I'm wondering why you're still here, Darius, why they haven't kicked your ass downstairs."

"You wanna know why?" Darius said. "I'll tell you why. It's because I save lives, and after all isn't that what He wants—to rescue a woeful world of worshiping humans? Who cares what I say, or how I look to those beasts? It's my actions that count, right? The humans say the road to hell is paved with good intentions, well my intentions might be a touch evil, but last week I saved close to five-thousand lives—that's why I'm still here."

Darius took a sip from a cup of coffee that was neither cold nor bitter—even though it'd been sitting out for several hours—one hundred and seventy degrees, optimum temperature for that beverage. He spat it on the floor.

"Fuck! How about a shitty cup of coffee once in a while? It's too fucking perfect here. I want a cloudy day when it's supposed to be bright. I want a storm when they've asked for calm. I'm done I tell you. I hate serving them."

Ezekiel put his hand on Darius's shoulder. He was brotherly and kind, understanding and radiated love.

"Darius, shut up. Take what they give you. Do as you're told and before you know it, it'll all be over. We've got another hundred years or so until He pulls the plug, and then you won't have to worry anymore. And believe me—if you think Lucifer's people have it any better, I can guarantee you that Baal is probably right now wishing he could get a cup of warm Joe instead of that cold bitter store-bought crap that they're serving below."

Darius laughed. "Well," he said "I do like my cup warm."

Ezekiel began to shimmer… "I got a call Darius, I gotta go."

He disappeared.

* * * * * * * * * * *

Darius took the elevator to the first floor and checked in at Angel Resources. He wasn't surprised that this office had suddenly appeared, or that "Angel Resources" now existed when a moment before it hadn't—that's how things were around here; if He thought you needed it, it appeared.

"Unless it was something that He didn't want to appear," Darius thought, *"and then you got shit."*

Darius walked up to the counter and checked in. The angel behind the desk was new. Darius didn't know her, and he wasn't interested in small talk.

"I need to see somebody," Darius said, "maybe, a shrink, or something. Do you have that sort of thing here?"

"Yes, Darius," she politely replied. "The doctor has been waiting for you. Go in."

Darius entered and ignoring the outstretched hand of the doctor he walked across the room, behind the large desk, and plopped his ass straight down into the doctor's large red leather chair—rather than taking his seat on the long couch that he knew was designated as the patients' "spot." The doctor, without argument, calmly sat on the sofa. He was everything a psychiatrist should be—if you were thinking of one; white hair framing an old man's face, silver-grey neatly trimmed beard, small round eyeglasses with gold wire frames, and a long clean white coat. The bluish skin and tended wings of an angel were also as Darius expected—he would not seek help from a human.

"Do you feel better now?" the doctor asked. "Are you relieved?"

"Better?" the angel said. "*What do you mean do I feel better? I just got here.*"

"Well," the doctor replied. "You came in and sat in the chair that you knew must be for me, so that had to give you a feeling of control—and even, if I dare say so, a certain sense of defiance and superiority. Isn't that what you're seeking? Do you feel satisfied?"

Darius stood and walked to the couch.

"Get up," he said. He pointed at the doctor's recently vacated chair. "Let's go Freud." He snapped his fingers and the doctor, without a word, switched seats with Darius.

The angel felt his anger rise. "No more games," Darius said. "I'm uncomfortable. Fix it."

"Whatever you say, *Darius*," the doctor said. "Now, what brings you here?"

The angel sat for a moment. He wasn't exactly sure why he was there, was there a precedent for this type of thing? Had an angel ever sought help before—especially, help of this nature?

"You're troubled, Darius," the doctor said. "Let it out. Go ahead, you can speak freely here."

"Okay," Darius said, "You want me to talk? I'll talk. I'm down there pulling wrinkled old crones out of the frying pan, for what? Who gives a fuck? Where do they even go when they die? You ever see one around here? And, for that matter, I'm sick of it. I'm tired of serving them, and I'm not gonna do it anymore."

The doctor smiled. "I understand, Darius."

"You understand?" The angel was furious. *"Who the fuck are you?* Are you down there, digging in that human shit? I don't smell the scent of man on you—have you ever even seen one? They're horrible. Do you know I almost let one die? Yeah, don't look so shocked—5,000 years of half-monkey ass wiping and I'm over it."

The doctor took off his glasses and cleaned them with his wing.

"Darius, have you ever felt for one of them?"

"What?" Darius said. "I'm telling you how I feel right now."

"No," the doctor said. "Have you ever cared?"

"Cared about what?" Darius asked.

"Their struggles, their pain, their loss—have you ever looked into their eyes when they break, it's beautiful."

"They're nothing," Darius said. "You're asking me if I care for *things*—as if they're in some way different from this coat or these pants that I possess. When they're done—just like my trousers, they're done, tossed out, and we get new ones. There's a seemingly unending stream of human filth that populates that planet, and you're asking me *if I grieve for them, if I feel loss, or want?* What are you fucking talking about?"

"Darius, He's very concerned about you—we all are."

"Concerned about me? Then why does He have me serving those fucks, those dull, dim-witted beasts? What the fuck do they do for Him? Did you know that some of us call them the dream-wreckers? Have you seen what they've done down there? They've made a mess of it."

"Darius, please, I know they're difficult—*He* knows they're difficult, but He was hoping that maybe, after all this time, you might…"

"I might what; learn to take it up the ass with a smile on my face?"

The doctor laughed. "Darius, I'm going to let you in on a secret, something that only a few of us know. God screwed up."

"What?" Darius said. He leaned forward on the couch.

"He screwed up." The doctor said. "Do you want to know why you're angry, why you don't see how He could care, and why you hate *them* so much? It's because He didn't create you with a built-in ability to love. We angels have to learn it, and you haven't— and when you don't have it, you sure as hell can't see it in anyone else, let alone them. Why do you think Lucifer had such a hard time? He didn't love either, Darius. When you were created, He forgot to put love in you, all He gave you was a desire to serve, and after awhile, service without love becomes slavery. No one wants to be a slave, not even an angel."

Darius sat quietly.

"*He* loves them Darius, and that's all you need to know."

There was a moment of uneasy heavenly quiet.

"Are you fucking kidding me?" Darius broke the stillness in the room. "This, is the help I get? *He loves them—you don't.* And now I'm supposed to go back there and keep it up? I won't do it. I'm not taking another fucking call."

"Well, you could learn how to love," said the doctor. "That would make the service and the understanding easier, but that hurts, too. If I were you, I'd just shut up, and keep serving. Listen to your friend Ezekiel, and if you get a little loose with a few of the humans, so what." The doctor smiled, "I'm sure *He'll* forgive you."

Darius began to shimmer—he was being called and there

was nothing he could do.

"Nice talking with you, Darius—have a wonderful day."

Darius disappeared.

* * * * * * * * * * *

It was another random save—a young human child thoughtlessly ran in front of an auto. Darius did his job—sort of. He saved the child from dying, but he did let the boy get hit, and he laughed as the young body cart-wheeled across the intersection. Darius caught the child's head before it bounced off the pavement, and miraculously—according to the human witnesses, the boy walked away relatively unharmed—save for a few minor scratches.

"I don't get it," Darius said, "this love thing. I would have thought that if He really loved the kid, He would have let me kill the driver—or at least stop the boy from darting in front of a car." Darius sighed. "Love—what is love anyway, an emotion in which you let the failings in others fade into non-existence? Is that what love is? That you care nothing about their frailties and their weaknesses, and you ignore the fact that they just aren't good enough or strong enough to exist? Where is the perfection in that? Where is the glory in loving those who are not fit to be loved? I cannot learn to lessen myself, so that those beneath me may rise."

Darius moved among the people—unseen, unsettled, and gliding in no heavenly rhythm. He stopped on the corner of 51st and Bay—hovered above the street, and watched as a herd of men crossed on the green light. The city air was soiled with their petty conversations—deep clouds of black thought pain rising from their minds and drifting toward their Maker.

"They are nothing more than fearful beasts," Darius thought, as he listened to their minds. *"Or maybe, they're sad, tortured little clowns, created perfectly for the amusement of Him,"* he smirked, *"our most wonderful Lord."*

A young woman on crutches hobbled beneath Darius—her deformity, twisted and warped.

"Really?" Darius said. He reached down and touched the rough curve of her spine as she passed. She groaned in pain. "He loves this—how quaint."

Darius drifted to the ground and then held up his hand, palm out, his long fingertips reaching toward the stars. A man stopped before him. He wore the uniform of a city worker—orange jumpsuit, pants cuffed over thick black rubber boots. The man had recently been in the sewer. His hands fouled by the grime that lay beneath the streets. He couldn't see the obstruction of Darius—he thought he had paused to think and rest—but his mind was displayed like a vibrant life painting pinned to the corners of the city street, shamelessly unfurled before the angel.

"What could He possibly see in one so foul?" Darius wondered. *"It surely cannot be in their looks."* The angel pushed the man's greasy hair away from his face and then he wrapped the locks in his fist and held him still. *"Their works have brought no joy to this world. They may at times comfort each other, but they do so to heal the wounds that they themselves brought on. I will give no praise to those who take pride in softening a harm that others of their kind created—they are all guilty, and not one rises above the rest."*

Darius looked into the man. The worker was troubled— worried about his daughter. She was in poor health, plagued by the evils in her mind—melancholia, hysteria. Darius followed the man's thoughts as they led through the city and into the bedroom of the young girl. She was asleep in the man's dream, drugged and resting quietly—the only time she seemed at peace.

Darius held the thought in place as he stepped through the man's mind and into the bedroom of the girl. It was exactly as her father pictured—a young maid's room—pink, and fairy light, the only hint to the madness lying under the covers was a stack of paintings on the desk—brilliant, tortured, oil-colored-screams, reflecting the terrors of her dreams. Darius was surprisingly and uncharacteristically moved.

"Maybe it's all this talk of love," he thought, *"but I can almost feel her pain."*

He lifted the painting and admired the strokes drawn by her trembling hand—a seascape aswim with death and loss. *"She paints like an angel. Look how she's captured the essence of the ocean, the unselfish dangers of the sea."*

Darius lifted another, and then held still as night, for there, splashed across the canvas, in fire blues and deep sea greens, were his eyes. The very likeness of Darius, chained to her work.

"What madness is this?" he said. "What trick of God comes here?"

Darius cocked his head in wonder, and then worry. *"This painting could mean trouble. I could be watched from on high—it does happen, not as much as one might think, but sometimes God does take an interest in those who serve him. The doctor did say they were worried, and if that were the case, there could be another angel following my path."* Darius instantly transported himself to the street, and then in a flash to the roof, the hallway outside the door, and then, the closet next to her bed, but there was no one there. He was alone, except for the girl lying silently beneath the flowered covers. Darius spoke out, just in case.

"Yes, I do dislike them," Darius said aloud, "but I enjoy this job, and I'm really going to try and learn this 'love' thing—it sounds like a great idea." Darius, amidst all his grumblings, did not want to be sent down—it was the coffee that did it. *"I'd rather be unhappy with a sweet, warm cup,"* he reasoned, *"than unhappy with a bitter, cold one."*

Darius, now satisfied that he'd covered his angelic ass, walked to the bed and gently lifted the blanket. She was sleeping on her stomach—her face buried in the pillows. Darius reached down and tenderly put his finger beneath her chin. He turned her face toward him.

Her skin, teen-age blemished-alabaster radiated translucent light. She lit the room like a candle that lay upon the breast of God. She was beautiful—a human carved from the ripe flesh of madness. The girl opened her eyes.

"Oh…" The angel exhaled what could only be described as the noise of a small pain, but in an instant the heaviness of the world descended upon him and he was crushed by its weight. He became solid, fell to the ground, and was stranded on earth in his heavenly form—an angel, pulled by his newfound love through the gates of heaven and dumped on the soft pile carpeting of a young girl's room.

She sat upright in her bed, her long red hair flowing over the sheets that she'd pulled to her chin.

"Hello?" she said. "Man? Are you okay?"

Darius was dazed. He struggled to lift his head. He was unaccustomed to the weight of his now physical self. A fledgling bird fallen from the nest, he floundered.

"Man?" she called again. "Are you okay?"

"Help," Darius whispered. "Please, help me."

The girl didn't move—the shadows of her illness painted circles around the brilliant green windows of her soul—deathly shadows.

"Please," Darius begged. He managed to raise his arm. He reached for her.

The girl climbed naked from her bed. She was seventeen, barely a woman—and due to her mental state was more child than adult, but she knelt beside Darius and helped him sit up. The angel, slowly gaining strength, wrapped his great wings around the girl and pulled her close. It was the first time that he'd ever tenderly held a human, and the scent of her—the sweet perfume of her sweat—called to him. Darius stuck out the tip of his tongue and gingerly tasted her skin. She was clean and slightly salty, but when he slid his tongue down under her arm he grimaced and shook his head—her deodorant was metallic and unpleasant to his mouth.

"I know you," the girl said—she was not afraid of the angel; if anything, his appearance was a strange comfort to her and she laid her head against his chest. "I paint pictures of you," she said, "there, on the desk. You've come to me at night. You're an angel."

Darius said nothing. He'd never been here before. She couldn't know him. The new sensation of her skin thrilled him, as he let his hands roam freely over the girl's flesh, and there was no place on her that he did not touch. Each sweet inch he ingested in his mind, memorizing the slight curves of her breasts, the territory of her self.

"Are you real?" she asked, doing nothing to stop his hands.

"I'm not sure what you mean by real," Darius said, and then he remembered her illness. "I am with you in this place. I am flesh. This is no dream to be broken."

Darius lifted his hand to his mouth and bit through the skin.

He had never bled before. He held the wound toward the girl—bright red drops cascading to the carpet. She grabbed his hand, covered the wound with her mouth and suckled the blood until it stopped. She smiled up at Darius with lips now stained.

"Are you mine?" she said.

The concept of ownership was unfamiliar to Darius, but he knew that these humans often attached to one another and, when he searched inside himself, the thought of being owned by this young girl was not strange or unpleasant.

"Yes," Darius said. "I will be yours."

Their bodies locked in tight embrace, punctuated only by slight hand movements and flutters; they secured and then readjusted their hold. For some time they sat, oblivious to the world. Darius grew strong.

"Can I see you?" she asked, as she removed his jacket and unbuttoned his shirt. "I've never seen a man without his clothes. You are a man, aren't you?"

Darius wasn't sure. He was not himself, but he was not her either. He lifted the girl from him and then raised himself to his full height. He was seven feet tall, a span meant to symbolize an arm of God, one-third of a Holy image. He kicked off his shoes and then removed his shirt and pants. He stood naked before the girl, then shook and spread his wings—the tips of which reached from wall to wall.

The girl, still unclothed, moved closer to Darius and held her hands out to him. She touched the angel's chest and then slid her fingers down to his hips. She placed her hand on the smooth mound between the angel's legs.

"I don't think you're quite a man," she told him. "You don't have anything, here." She gently stroked. "You're like a doll," she said, "a great, blue doll."

Darius felt proud. He could sense delight in her assessment of him.

"Do you have a name?" she asked. "I'm Emily." She held out her small hand.

Darius reached out and gently wrapped her hand in his.

"Emma-Lee-Graves—Emily for short," she said.

"I am Darius. This name comes with nothing else, just Darius, as it's been forever."

"Darius…" she whispered, caressing the name with her lips, "I like it. Will you stay here with me?"

The angel thought for a moment. Could he still move, could

he fly? Darius concentrated on the street outside. He closed his eyes and imagined himself standing on the pavement looking back at the girl's house. He didn't move. He was still there—naked, standing on the carpet.

"Yes," he said. "I will stay with you."

"Forever?"

"Yes," pledged Darius, "I will stay forever."

Emily smiled and walked over to the nightstand. She picked up a small metal box.

"I like my songs sad, sweet, and full of love," she said, "like a warm night rain falling on the flowers outside."

The angel watched as she held the shiny rectangle in her left hand, the fingers on her right gliding across a smooth glass face. She found what she was looking for, "Last Goodbye," and set the small box down.

"I love to dance, Darius."

Music filled the room and to Darius it was beautiful, just as she said. He could feel the pain emanating from the vibrations of the song, but also, there was hope. The sadness wasn't futile or depressed; it was...Darius searched for the words..."It was a kiss goodbye." He'd seen it before, two humans when they separate,

pushing their lips together, then breaking their connection, and yet, in some way, celebrating their love at the same time. Darius watched Emily move. She swayed with the music, reminding him of the night flowers. She was one of them, moving in the torn breeze of the sound. Emily danced toward Darius. She took his hands and encouraged him to move—to sway like she did. The angel closed his eyes and imagined he was her, moving across the carpet, swaying in rhythm, a flower in the night, and then he too moved with the song. Emily sang along with the words, and through her Darius began to understand the beauty in the pain…

"Just hear this and then I'll go. You gave me more to live for…more than you'll ever know."

"It is loss," Darius thought. *"But it's finding, too. This song is as beautiful as she, as imperfect. Yes, her skin is blemished and her mind is touched, true, but I love her, and even more so because she is flawed. She is the rain; she is my storm and my sun. I love her beauty and I love her disease. She is everything to me; she is my reason to serve, my reason to…"*

"EMILY!" The door to the room had opened and there, standing in the doorway, was her father—the worker from the city.

"GET AWAY FROM IT!" he yelled.

Her father ran toward the couple, pushed at Darius and grabbed the girl's arm. He tried to pull her away, but the angel did as he had for thousands of years—he instinctively reached out, and he saved her. Darius grabbed the girl's father by his neck, and he broke him. He fell lifeless to the floor.

Darius kept dancing.

"DADDY!" the girl screamed and dropped next to her father. "DARIUS!" she yelled. "WHAT DID YOU DO?"

Darius opened his eyes and stopped swaying.

"I saved you," Darius calmly replied. "I love you." He beamed at the girl, ignoring the body on the floor.

"HELP ME!" she screamed. She tried lifting her father but his head fell forward on to his chest, his neck was snapped at the base. "Darius!" she stood and pulled at the angel. "Do something!"

Darius prodded the body with his foot. "I can't," he said. "He's not in there. I'm not sure where they go, but he's not in there."

"Darius, what are you saying?"

"There's no one there." He kicked at the body again, "It's… nothing." Darius closed his eyes and swayed.

"WHAT ARE YOU DOING?" she screamed.

"I'm moving, dancing like you do. Come with me." He held out his hands, pulling the girl to her feet.

"STOP IT!" she yelled. Darting back and forth between Darius and her father. "Help me!"

"I did help you." Darius said. "I helped us. He's gone. We can dance now, and we can kiss." He reached for her again but then, the music stopped. Darius wanted more.

Emily grabbed her phone and dialed the number for the police. Darius grabbed the small metal box and attempted to restart the song.

"9-1-1, what is your emergency?" the voice was professional, calm.

"Please," she yelled. "He killed my father! Help me! Help me!"

Darius held the metal box toward her.

"Help me," he said. "Could you make the sounds come again? Are they in there, too?" Darius leaned over and tried to put his ear to her phone.

"Hello?" the emergency operator said. "Are you there?"

Emily yanked the phone away. "Help!" she yelled. She backed away from Darius—he followed.

"Please, Emily," Darius grinned, "the song."

The girl grabbed the box and hit replay. The song flared to life. Darius swayed.

"Hello..." the operator said, "...are you there?"

"I'm here! I'm here!" Emily yelled. She ran from the room.

"Miss, I need you to calm down. Where are you? Is the assailant still there?"

"Yes," Emily cried. "He killed my father! Help!"

"We have officers on the way. Stay on the phone until they arrive."

Darius felt sad when Emily left the room—it was almost as if the sun now refused to shine. He wanted a kiss goodbye as *'That's what lovers do when they leave, they kiss goodbye.'*

He followed. Darius wandered down the hallway and into the living room of her small house, calling her name.

Emily was still on the phone. Darius came toward her.

"I want a kiss," he said, "a sad, pretty kiss goodbye."

"Stay away from me!" she yelled as she backed toward the front door of the house. Darius moved toward her.

"But I miss you when you're gone. I love you Emily!"

"Go away, I hate you! You're a monster. You killed my father."

Darius started to cry. He reached up and touched his cheek, felt the wetness, and caught a tear on his finger. He tasted it; it was salty like she was. He held his tear-stained finger out to her. "Look how I hurt. Look Emma Lee Graves, Emily for short, look how I hurt."

The girl, still naked, went through the door to the outside and Darius followed.

"I forgive you," he said. "I know you don't mean it—you love me too."

A police cruiser pulled up to the house, then another and another. Officers jumped from their cars, guns drawn and pointed at the naked angel. The girl ran toward them. Darius stood tall, still crying.

"Get down on the ground," an officer ordered, but the angel would not stop. He advanced toward the girl, toward the officers, toward their guns.

"Stop!" The officer shouted. "We will shoot."

Darius captured another tear from his cheek, and carefully balancing it on his finger, he held it out and continued toward the girl. "Look Emily, look at me hurt."

The first bullet tore through his chest, the second his stomach—the third, fourth, and fifth, back to his chest. Darius dropped to his knees—the warm day breeze weaved its way through the holes in his body.

"I love you, Emily. I love you."

He crawled toward her, tried to rise, but was hit by shots six and seven. His knee was shattered, a bullet tumbling through his shoulder slightly under his wing.

Darius collapsed. He was conscious for a moment and then the world wavered and became still.

"Darius…Darius? Can you hear me?" It was Ezekiel. "Are you done now? Have you had enough?"

"Please don't take me. I love her."

The police advanced with taser and club.

"It's time to go Darius," he said. "Come on."

Ezekiel held out his hand and reluctantly Darius grabbed it. The angels vanished.

* * * * * * * * * * *

"So that's love, huh?" Darius said. "It was awful."

"Yeah," Ezekiel said, "I could've told you that, but you wouldn't listen."

"You know," Darius went on. "Maybe He didn't give us that ability on purpose, maybe He didn't fuck up. Maybe, He did it to protect us."

"Maybe who did it?" Ezekiel asked. "Did what? What ability? What are you talking about?"

"I'm talking about love. The doctor said God screwed up. He didn't give us the ability to love, and that's why I was so angry. He said I was a slave."

"And you believed him?"

"Yeah, of course I did, why not?"

"I'll tell you Darius, you may do great works, but you're a fool of the highest order—tricked into love and too blind to see it."

"He was a doctor with an office and a couch, he told me so."

Ezekiel smiled, "And to Adam he was a snake, and to Christ he was a word. Have you been back to see her, checked in on her, cruised by her bed at night?"

Darius hung his head. "Yes," he said. "I was thinking that maybe if I tried again, was a little more understanding, softer, or more kind, that maybe things might work out."

"Darius, you murdered her father. She called the police on you. They tried to kill you."

"Yeah, she did," Darius said, "but she also said she loved me, and she looks so beautiful when she dances."

Ezekiel began to shimmer. "I've got to go; I've got a call to take, but Darius…"

"Yeah, Zeke?"

"I love you."

A Late Night Session

It wasn't a loud knock—more of a light tap-tap, but it was enough to get me out of bed and to my feet. At first, I thought it was a prank—some errant children playing late-night door ditch-'em games, for when I gazed outside, no one was there—at least, no one at eye, or even waist level—and as I was about to withdraw, shut the door, and return to bed, a small, cute, cuddle-me-up-on-the-blanket voice, spoke from below my knees. It was a rabbit—a child's stuffed toy standing white fur distressed on my porch.

"May I?" the bunny said as it stepped into my home. "It's frightfully cold outside, and he's being most impolite—terribly so."

She had brown woodland eyes, and it looked as if she'd been crying; her cheeks were tear-stained and matted.

"We need help," the bunny said, "and we saw your sign."

I was a therapist—a family counselor—but I didn't work

with toys.

I began to shut the door when a voice called from outside—a deep, raspy growl.

"I told her it wasn't true, but she wouldn't listen—never listens, unless it's something that she thinks she wants to hear." The

voice came from a bear; a two-foot tall teddy, laboriously making his way, one stuffed leg at a time, up and on to my porch.

"This was her idea," he said, "not that I'm against it, but I told her, that if you'd just listen to me, we wouldn't have to be out on a night like this."

He was very chatty for a bear, and the night was not pleasant—it was a desperate evening of wind and rain. I held the door, and he too crossed the threshold of my home.

"I don't normally see people at night," I said.

The bear growled.

"But we're not people, and we only come out at night. How would it be, the two of us, walking about in broad daylight with her crying and complaining? I don't see what help you're going to be if you can't see the troubles in that."

"I'm not saying…"

"He's not saying anything at all, Bear," said the bunny. "You won't let *him* speak, just as you won't let *me* speak. You don't want me to be what I am. You don't want me to have a voice!" The bunny began to cry. "You want a body, a warm body to rub up against. But I'm more than that…I'm so much more."

The bear hung his head, mumbled a slight apology, and then

looked up at me with chipped green button eyes. This was an old bear, a bear with years of before-bedtime wear.

"It's quite okay," I said, as I led them deeper into my home. "We can sit here—anywhere you'd like."

I kept a small room that I used as an office. The walls were painted a warm goldenrod. There was an over-stuffed couch and a chair. It was a comfortable room, a room to relax and to let go. The bunny and the bear sat next to each other on the sofa—a pillow placed strategically between the two. The bear looked nervous. He was obsessively running his paw over the arm of the couch, pushing and squeezing the fabric.

"Are you comfortable?" I asked him.

"Yes, comfortable," he said. "I was just wondering what kind of stuffing you have in this couch." His arm was slightly torn and seemed to have lost a bit of its filling. "It's very nice," he said, "very nice."

"So, what brings the two of you here?" I asked.

"That's just it," the bunny cried. "It's not 'two', it's one. It's always him, him, him. I'm no one when he's around." The bunny spoke in a voice that reminded me of a soft church bell—a small broken heaven voice.

"You're not nobody; you're Bunny," the bear grumbled beneath his breath. "*You think you're nobody*, that's the problem."

The bunny rounded on me with dark pleading eyes. "Bear is not a therapist, if anything he's a hypnotist—a charmer. Don't listen to him. He lies and people believe him. They always believe him. Nobody ever believes me."

"That's not true," The bear growled and then caught himself. "I don't lie. Well, I do lie, but I don't lie about the things that matter, I don't lie about the truth."

The bear *was* strangely believable.

"You see," the bear, said, "she does these things and then blames me. She was shuffled from child to child—she never got close to anyone. I listen to her. I beg her to speak. She blames me for a lifetime of what others have done. I'm not a monster. I'm a bear, a big cuddly bear. I just want to love her, but she's making it most difficult."

The bunny had been quiet as the bear spoke, but now she shook and shivered with anger.

"He's a liar!" she yelled. "I saw him! He was on her bed, the older girl, and he was nestled in her arms snuggling, and cuddling. She kissed him—right on the lips! And he let her!"

"I did not!" the bear roared.

He stood on the couch—his great tufted paws aloft, looming over the bunny in a most threatening manner. "You're the one!" he growled. "Where did all those little bunnies come from? There was just you and now, bunnies everywhere—hundreds of bunnies on the bed!"

The bear lumbered toward her.

"STOP!" I yelled.

He held his place but turned and looked at me with a savage forest stare.

"Please," I said. "Please, Mr. Bear, be calm and breathe. Please."

The bear settled and then plopped down on his well-padded bottom. He slowly, resignedly shook his head.

"I know what she is," he said softly, "and I don't mind her nature, if only she would not mind mine. I know she can't help herself. Try her."

"What?" I said.

"Try her." He gestured toward the bunny.

The bunny's face had changed. Her eyes swirled with lust. She leaned back on the couch and seductively spread her legs.

"Touch her," The bear coaxed. "Go ahead and touch her."

I was strangely compelled to lean over, and I ran my hand along the side of her face—gently stroking her fur. She pushed into me.

"Hold her," the bear commanded.

I picked up the bunny and held her against my face. She nuzzled into my neck and tiny-bunny-kissed my cheek.

"Take me," she whispered.

I'd never felt attraction like this—a lust that went beyond reason. I needed her and I didn't care that the bear was watching— standing now on the sofa, intent on our contact, directing our play. I put the bunny in my lap and she wiggled against me—moving her hips as a woman would with desire and purpose.

"Let me hold her for you." The bear climbed down from the sofa and grabbed the bunny. He carried her to the couch and laid her on her back—her legs spread, eyes closed.

"Do it," he said. "She wants this. This is what she's made for."

I undid my pants and got down on my knees before the pair. I held her small legs and I pushed against and then inside her.

"Bite me," the bunny whispered to the bear. The bear leaned

down, kissed, and then lightly bit her neck.

"Watch me, Bear," she purred, "watch me fuck him."

The bear watched as I pushed deeper, moving within her. I felt her breath against me—the perfume of dark cinnamon nights and wild childhood kisses. It was as if she was made for me, sewn from the fabric of all I had ever desired. I came, releasing into the toy.

The bunny leaned back and passionately kissed her bear. He returned her kiss in kind. I was dazed and ashamed.

"I'm sorry." I said. "I don't know what came over me."

The bunny righted herself on the couch—calm, relaxed, and without the slightest care.

"It's okay," said the bear. "She's a good bunny, but she's a bunny, and I don't blame her for that—as long as she doesn't blame me for being a bear." He picked her up and walked towards the door—the bunny, cradled in his arms, relaxed and tired, like a child peacefully falling asleep.

"You were very good," said the bear, "and we'll be back—it won't be long before she gets troubled again. We'll need your help."

The bear put the bunny over his shoulder, opened the door, and walked off into the night.

Something to Burn

When the grocery store on South Spring turned to ashes in the parking lot, Terrance was across the street sipping on a soft drink soda and fiddling with the radio station. His car was without tape or CD capabilities, and probably, as he figured, one of the last vehicles to come off the assembly line with only an AM/FM player. *"Do you know how hard it is to find the proper arson-accompanying music on commercial radio?"* He'd flipped through numerous channels, even trying a few of the Mexican stations, before he finally settled on a late night talk show. He didn't care what they were going on about— politics mostly—but the monotonous, boring voices perfectly offset the imploding store—*"Tonight's roaring blaze is being brought to you live by the soothing tones of W.K.N.B."*

Terrance knew this burn was going to be good, and it didn't disappoint. You see, although the building was in a shopping mall, it stood apart from the other stores—plenty of room on both sides for ventilation, and lots of windows; the more windows the better. It was nice to be able to look inside while that rambunctious little flame so rudely danced down the aisles, tickling the canned goods on number nine before leaping over to aisle twelve and incinerating the laxatives and the foot powder. There is nothing more satisfying than seeing your handiwork come to life, and Terrance had been satisfied many times—three times this month. It was always uplifting. But... he was getting a trifle bored—the newlywed shine was wearing off the flames and he thought it might be nice to step it up a notch, add a new element; perhaps insert a figure or two into the picture—a ménage à trois of sorts. *"How would it be,"* he wondered, *"to watch a man trying to escape the flames—or a woman for that matter? How long would it take before they went the way of the tissues and the frozen foods?"* It was an exciting thought. Terrance sat back in his seat and tapped his fingers on the steering wheel—*"Burn, baby, burn."*

Terrance had hoped that tonight's view would be a clear one, and he'd gotten his wish. The flame danced slowly for him, and the fire's lecherous patron—that cloud of loose smoke that hung around and tried to block his view of the action—was well behaved. He didn't mind the smoke as long as it stayed on top, where it belonged, like a cherry on top of a sundae, but when it filled the building, it was hard to see the burn. *"Cherry on top, that's right, you don't want cherry all over, just on top—like smoke, on top, where it belongs."* He checked his watch and realized he was about 40 minutes away from getting fired—that is, if he didn't get back to his job.

Terrance was a night watchman—not a security guard—let's make that perfectly clear. He despised authority and anything to do with the law. *"People should be free to come and go as they please,"* he thought, *"but they should be watched."* Terrance's job was perfect—paid shit; boring as hell if he stayed around, but wonderful for what he loved doing best—watching, and starting fires. How lucky for him that his employment contributed to his leisure time enjoyment. *"It's a rare thing,"* Terrance smiled, *"loving your job as much as I do. I should thank someone."*

Terrance returned to his place of employment, Hedge's Self Storage. He drove to the back of the building. A dark blue Crown Victoria that "did not belong in the lot" was parked between spaces, and it was occupied. Terrance, although not an abnormally agitated man, was concerned, he *had* been off premises and he didn't want to lose his situation. The last thing he needed was to be forced to find another job, at the very untalented and unemployable age of 51. He thought of a thousand different excuses to explain his absence, including one where he actually defecated in his pants—*"No one questions a man's inability to perform when he's carrying a hot load in his slacks."*

"But, maybe the car isn't a threat," Terrance thought. *"This lone sedan occupant might not be a company man at all. Maybe, it's just some drunk sleeping it off on a deserted blacktop hideaway. Yeah, that's what it is, a drunk, too inebriated to drive. The bars had recently closed. This is when they come out. Yes, it must be a drunk, and he would need to be watched."*

In the space of a few moments, Terrance had turned a perceived threat into an opportunity to use his night watchman skills. *"I'll give the guy credit for not driving, but I'll be damned if he's going to lay up in here, puking and pissing in my lot."*

Terrance pulled directly behind the blue sedan and slammed on his brakes. He then power-jumped his way from the driver's seat, hitched up his smoke-saturated, yet still unsoiled size 28 polyester patrol pants, stood as tall as his five foot six small-boned frame allowed, and made ready to watch. She was out of the car before he could get settled. She had a gun. Terrance did not.

"Nice night for it, huh?" she was calm—a quick mover, but calm—and less concerned with her .45 caliber hand accouterment than Terrance was. It was the first thing he noticed, hard steel nestled casually at her waist. "Of course," she continued, "a quick burn in a light rain can also be quite stunning. What do you have," she glanced at her watch, "about 20 minutes before the day man gets here?"

Terrance said nothing. He was too busy watching his job, and his life, go up in flames.

"Oh, don't get me wrong," she said. "I'm a big fan of your work. I especially loved what you did to the sporting goods on West 75th—now, *that* was nice."

"I'm sure I don't know what you're talking about," Terrance said. "I'm a watchman, a night watchman, and, uh, you shouldn't be here."

She advanced toward him. Terrance stepped back. She had at least four inches on him, and maybe 50 pounds.

"You're telling me where I should be, little man? If I were you, I'd be worrying about where *you're* going to be." She opened her jacket and flashed Terrance the badge that she wore on her hip— neatly clipped to a thin black belt holding up her slacks.

"It is slacks, isn't it?" Terrance wondered out loud. "Do

women wear pants?"

Terrance caught his thoughts and apologized, "I'm sorry, I didn't mean anything. We're on the same team, right?"

The woman laughed. "Oh, you're on my team, are you?"

She wore a black leather jacket—more tailored than he would've thought appropriate on an officer, and her breasts were large, barely concealed behind a white button-down blouse.

"We'll see whose team you're on," she said.

She holstered the gun and pulled a pack of cigarettes from her coat pocket, opened them and placed one on top of the thick coating of bright red lipstick that adorned her mouth. The cigarette sunk down into the glossy paste until it settled on her lip. She pulled out a lighter and brought it to the tip of the smoke, cupped it with her left hand and then spun her right thumb along the wheel—a smooth click and a flash. Terrance wistfully inhaled the butane as he watched her hands glow. He unconsciously maneuvered himself to get a better look at the tiny blaze. She lit the smoke and slowly pulled the lighter away. The flame was undisturbed by the cool night air. Terrance followed the lighter with his eyes as she circled the still-burning tool down to her waist and then back up to her face where she snap-closed the top, killing the flame and leaving Terrance to

stare directly into her eyes. He shook his head clear.

"Yeah," she said, "you really love it, don't you?" She took a deep lung-expanding drag and then exhaled a thick white cloud in Terrance's direction where, untouched by the smoke, he coughed anyway.

"I'm sorry." he stuttered, "Are you an officer? Am I being charged with something?"

"I don't know," she gave a casual television cop reply, "maybe arson. How does that sound, little 'fire-bug'?"

"I didn't do anything," Terrance said. "I was here all—"

"—Night? I watched you pull in. Were you about to lie to me?" She closed the gap between them and grabbed the back of his neck. Terrance tried to shrug her off but she pulled him close. He could smell the smoke on her breath, the leather of her coat, and a light trace of perfume or body lotion on her skin. Her cold manicured nails pressed into his flesh. She squeezed, hard.

"You're not gonna do fuck-all," she said. "I've been watching you, and I know where you've been. You're in trouble Terrance. That is your name isn't it—T. Terrance Boyd? Was your father black? Because it sounds like you gotta bit of brother in you; do you?" she reached down to his crotch and squeezed.

"Hey!" Terrance pushed her hand away. "What the fuck?"

"I thought you were on my team, baby."

Terrance rechecked the badge on her hip. This woman was certifiable, and she was armed. He sniffed the air searching for that too-much-to-drink odor, but it wasn't there—just perfume and cigarettes.

"I bet you're wondering how I found you."

Terrance wasn't. He was wondering about his job, the burning end of her smoke, and whether she could zip that jacket up with all those titties underneath. Terrance had seen more fires than he had sexual action, and that crotch grab, albeit unasked for, was thrilling.

"It wasn't hard," she continued. "Bugs like you love your work. We knew we had an arsonist, so I figured that you were probably watching. I'd roll on 451s and cruise the perimeters. I didn't own any of the buildings you were torching, so I wasn't in any real rush to stop you. After a couple of big fires, there you were, sitting in that old piece of shit Ford with a just-eaten-dinner shit-satisfied grin on your face—a grin that definitely doesn't belong in *that* car." She gestured to his '76 Fiesta. "I didn't need to look twice to know it was you. No one would sit in that piece of shit and smile, if their mind weren't occupied with something else. Isn't that right, Terrance?"

She was right, and despite his fear of being arrested, the woman's warm breath and tight grip had caused Terrance to become erect—embarrassingly so.

"What do you want from me?" he asked. He put his hands in his pockets and pulled his pants away from his cock—he didn't have far to pull. "I don't want any trouble. I want to be helpful and…"

"…Not go to jail?" she asked.

"Yeah," Terrance said. "I don't want to go to jail."

She let her cigarette drop. Terrance followed its descent. It met the ground with a small explosion of sparks. It was beautiful, *"Even on a small scale, fire can be so grand."*

She checked her watch. It was a nice piece, looked expensive with a large dial—the kind of watch that was usually made for men—a man's watch.

"I'm going to do you a favor, 'little bug'. Would you like that?" she asked.

Terrance nodded.

"I'm gonna save your ass, but first, you're going to do something for me. You do *want* to be on *my* team, don't you?"

She pulled a slip of paper out of her jacket pocket and handed it to him. An address was scrawled in fine red ink. "I want you to go check this out. See what you can do with it. There's a hill on the top of Olive, one street over—a vacant lot with a great view...and, Terrance?"

"Yes, ...um...uh." He didn't get her name.

"Check it before Friday. I'll be back then." She opened her car door and nodded at his Fiesta. "Move that piece of shit, and don't wander off. I'm watching you."

She pulled out of the lot as the day man pulled in.

* * * * * * * * * * *

The neighborhood was upscale—wandering manicured gardens and architecturally designed houses. Great pines lined the streets. At times their boughs created a thick forest canopy over the road. Fires loved these hillside neighborhoods. A good burn could take days to extinguish. Terrance had been here before. Last summer he'd thought about doing a piece of work in this area, but at the time of his reconnaissance, he was still fairly new and he didn't want to be too bold. He thought it would be best to work his way up, not get ahead of himself, and show a little humility. *"These days people aren't willing to put the time in, everybody wants to be a big shot—burn the whole city down on their first go around. What was the matter with starting on a row of dumpsters or a carport?"* That's how he cut his teeth, with a few garage fires. Yeah, his last drive through he'd thought about it, but he had the humility of a student, admiring what could be, not a brute, looking for undeserved glory.

Terrance thought back to his first burn—a single-car garage—part of an old abandoned house near the airport. It began as a small fire, but it went quick, and it spread, enveloping two more houses and a corner market in its wake before it came to rest. As a special treat, the runway near the burn had to be closed. *"You see, you start off with a bit of humility and you get rewarded."*

But Terrance was past that now. He drove down the street as a master; surveying the materials available before he began his creation.

The lot on Olive was just as she said; he had an unobstructed view across the gully to the back windows of Three-Thirty-Six Sand Canyon Drive—the address she'd scrawled on the paper. It was nice, a real clean setup. The house was perched on a steep hillside—stilts supporting the rear.

"How wonderful," Terrance thought. *"It was almost as if the architect wanted it to be torched. It was plump and perched on the*

hillside screaming, 'Burn me, burn me!' It couldn't be better."

Terrance imagined what it would look like when the stilts gave way. When the house exploded like a flaming wooden comet down the hillside.

"Yes, this is going to be nice."

The threat of jail and loss of job had been pushed aside as

the fantasy of the fire weaved its way about him. He was all business now. He surveyed the neighbor's homes—would there be lookie-loos to spoil his fun? There were a couple of windows, sure—lots of windows, but this being a high-digit area, he doubted whether anyone was too concerned about their neighbors.

"That is the good thing about these places—stuffy hill-dwellers with money who wanted to live with a 'close to', but 'outside-the-city' feel. Most of them don't associate with those around them— being too familiar with the neighbors decreased the feeling of privacy. No one should get too nosey."

Terrance was about to pull away when a light in the rear of the house came on. It looked like a bedroom. A pretty young blonde entered followed by…*"Shit! It's her. The cop from last night."* Immediately Terrance's worries about jail and the reality of his situation returned. *"Does she know I'm watching?"*

Terrance ducked down in his seat as if it would somehow make his car less visible.

The young girl walked to the window and pulled the drapes closed. Terrance fired up the Fiesta. He put the car in gear, made ready his departure, but then, the drapes reopened. This time there was no blonde. The threatening cop bitch was framed between the curtains. She looked directly at Terrance and a smile slowly spread across her face, like a line of petrol delicately laid upon a bedspread. Terrance turned off the car. He sat, a varmint caught in her sights.

She stepped away and the lights lowered. The room darkened to a soft evening glow. Terrance held. Momentarily, she returned to the window with the young girl in tow. They stood where Terrance could see them—two, almost silhouettes, framed behind the glass. The cop pulled the girl close and kissed her—a deep soulful kiss that rooted Terrance to his seat. She ran her hands down the girl's shoulders, unbuttoning her blouse, removing it, and then releasing the bra beneath.

Terrance watched as the cop stripped her naked and then knelt before her. She kissed the girl's stomach and then worked her way down between her legs.

"What the fuck? This bitch brings me out here to have me watch her go down on some chick?" Terrance started the car again but the crazy cop in the window heard his engine and held her hand up, wordlessly commanding him to stay in place. She didn't want him to leave. Terrance sat and watched as the cop took the young girl to what looked like completion and then the officer stood, moved to the window and closed the drapes.

"OK. I'm fucked. This bitch is crazy. I gotta get the fuck out of here…no, if I leave town she'll screw me, and I'm broke, fuck, I'm broke! I can't run, but she's gonna do me if I don't. She's fucking crazy. Does she even want the place torched? See, people like her, lots of people like her, just want to fuck with people. She just wants to fuck with me. She doesn't care. I wasn't hurting anyone. I certainly didn't hurt her—she even said it didn't hurt her. But now she's doing this, she's hurting me like this. She makes me see it, makes me sit here and I can't…"

"What the fuck are you doing?" the policewoman appeared at the driver's window startling Terrance out of his rambling monologue.

"I…I was checking it out, like you told me," Terrance stuttered.

"You were probably sitting out here jerking off, you creep," she reached through the window and grabbed at Terrance's crotch.

"Stop it! What do you want from me? Why are you doing this?"

"Easy, Romeo, lighten up. I'm just having some fun, giving you a little show, and you know what I want from you; I want you to do the place…with her in it."

"What?" Terrance asked

"You heard me." She said. "I want you to torch it. I don't care if the whole fucking hill goes with it, but I want it done—tomorrow."

"But I've never hurt anyone," he said. "And you were just with her—isn't she your…your…" Terrance fought for the word.

"My bitch?" The cop laughed. "She's a piece of ass, Terrance; a rich piece of ass, and I'm tired of it. I'm thinking I might switch teams, get me a little boy to play with—maybe you."

"You're sick," he said. "You need help!"

"I need help? Fucking firebug burning up half of LA and you tell me *I need help*. Listen here little bug. I could've done you in that parking lot last night, blown your fucking brains all over the back of Hedge's, and I would've been a hero, 'Female cop shoots male arsonist'."

She reached down and pulled the gun from her waistband. "Is that what I should've done, blown your fucking head off? I still can. I can say you found out I was investigating you and you followed me here, to kill me. I saw you outside, snuck up on you, identified myself and you resisted. So I shot you—'Bam'—right in the fucking head. That's a great story—straight HBO."

She pointed the gun toward Terrance's head. "How does that sound, bitch?"

"I'm sorry," Terrance said.

She pushed the gun against Terrance's cheek, the long muzzle caressing his pockmarked flesh. She slid it toward his mouth. "Open up little bug. Open up, I want you to suck on this." She pushed the gun against his lips. Terrance kept his mouth firmly closed.

"Open your fucking mouth or I'll shove it in, and break your fucking teeth." Terrance reluctantly opened. She pushed the barrel between his thin lips.

"Now be a good little bug and suck it." Terrance sucked on the barrel of the gun—the metal cold, leaving an acrid taste in his mouth.

"That's right," she cooed. "That's my little girl. But don't suck too hard." She laughed, "You wouldn't want to make her cum."

Terrance did as he was told, but as she said, not too hard.

"That a girl. Look at you go."

"Gina!" a woman's voice yelled from the hilltop. "Gina!"

She jerked the gun out of Terrance's mouth—chipping a tooth and cutting his lip on exit. She rubbed the wet barrel on the sleeve of his shirt.

"I gotta go," she said. "Get it done, little bug, or next time…"
She waved the pistol at him, "…she's gonna cum. Now get the fuck
out of here!" She slapped the side of his car and jogged up the hill.

* * * * * * * * * * *

Normally, Terrance rose at 4pm, had a quick breakfast of
grapefruit and wheat toast—lightly buttered—*real butter, not
spread,* before he left for work at 6pm, but not today. He'd awakened
early. His sleep had been uneasy—fitful. He'd been up and down all
night—and not just to urinate, something that he did on the average
of three times an evening, he was having dreams of that awful
woman. In the last dream: *he was kneeling before her, naked, his
ass exposed to the world, and he was sucking on her finger, licking
ants off the tip—nasty little red ants that marched off her hand and
drunkenly paraded down his throat. He could feel them sloshing
about in his stomach, screaming and vainly searching for a way out.*
He shook his head to clear his thoughts, and then he grabbed his car
keys and took the Fiesta for a drive. *"It really isn't such a bad car."*
He thought. *"Fuck her."*

Terrance was a simple man who liked fires and, other than
the illegalities associated with his hobby, he was a law abiding
citizen; paid his taxes, followed basic traffic rules and wasn't one to

imbibe of spirits.

Terrance took a wide turn on to Grand Avenue and headed downtown.

"Fires were pure and freeing," he thought. *"Not like being a policewoman, caging and stopping. I let things loose. I let flames dance, and embers sing. I'm a creator and a watcher, and she's just...what the fuck?"*

He swung the car about, turned right on 16th and then parked at the 7-11 on Lincoln. He thought he'd recognized a familiar face but he needed to be sure. From his vantage point he could easily see the indoor Mexican swap meet parking lot and the entrance to the stores. He was right; he did see someone he knew; it was that bitch cop, sitting in a chair near the front door, dressed in dark blue polyester, eating a fucking churro, and she was armed.

"She isn't a cop," Terrance thought. *"She's a guard, a fucking security guard for a swap meet. What the fuck? How did she know about me? How did she find me? Wait, wait, maybe she's off duty, moonlighting; but no, no. Look at her, she looks comfortable in that chair—she is a guard—fuckin' A."*

Terrance was furious, not only had he been scared near to death but also, she'd made him suck that gun, and who knew where it'd been.

"And she's armed, the bitch is armed; she's crazy and they let her have a gun! What is this world coming to?"

A man, seemingly of some importance, walked from the shops and confronted Terrence's nemesis. The man was yelling, and she was taking it, her shoulders slumped, her face sad, apologetic. Terrance was ecstatic. *"That bitch must have fucked up and now she's getting reamed. Ha! I hope he cans that cunt! Fire her! Come on! Fire her!"*

The man finished with his irritation, walked back the way he came—looking over his shoulder to make sure she was following, and then they both disappeared through the market's doors—she puppy-dog'd his heels.

"Ain't so bold now—Miss, grab-my-crotch. I hope he's giving you what you gave me. How's that gun taste bitch! Ha! That'd teach her!" It was 20 minutes before Terrance saw her again. He had been gleefully watching the front door, fantasizing about her being punished and he almost missed her. She'd exited the side of the building and Terrance rightly assumed that she had been fired.

"I wonder what she did?" he mused. *"Probably got caught bullying customers or gun diddling. I sure hope he took the pistol."*

Terrance pulled the collar of his jacket up and acted painfully nonchalant as he watched her drop her keys twice while attempting to enter her car. When finally seated, she pounded the steering wheel in anger. Terrance giggled. She started her vehicle, threw it into reverse and plowed into a shopping cart that tumbled over and got stuck beneath her bumper. This drew an all out guffaw from Terrence who then took the opportunity to run back to the 7-11 and retrieve his trusty Fiesta. He pulled around just in time to see her turn into traffic and drive off—her bumper noticeably scuffed.

Terrance followed, a few car lengths behind. He was good at being nondescript, invisible. He had always melted into the woodwork—at least until he had popped up on her radar. She drove toward the park on 7th and then turned into a rather run-down neighborhood near the channel. She parked in front of an old apartment building, exited her vehicle, walked up a flight of stairs and entered one of the units.

"This is more like it," Terrance thought. *"This is a place where a security guard might live, not a big ol' house in the hills. I wonder how she ended up there anyway, wrapped up with that blonde, sneaking around at night. I wouldn't be surprised if she bullied her too."*

Terrance checked his watch—not as nice as her piece—or as masculine, but it did the job. She was inside for a full hour before she walked down the stairs and got into her car. He was about to follow and pull in behind her, when she did a quick U-turn and headed back in his direction. He lay down in the front seat and held still. He didn't breathe for the first 15 seconds, but then he quickly exhaled, gasped, and held again. He expected a pounding on his door, or even a broken glass entry demanding an explanation for his presence, but there was none. She hadn't seen him, and after a generous while he sat up to a clear coast. She was gone.

Terrance decided to do some quick, safe recon. He walked up to the building, climbed the old concrete and metal staircase, got just high enough to see the number 6 on her door, and then he retreated, stopping only for a second to check the apartment complex's mailbox—number 6, G. Hernandez.

"Gina Hernandez," he said the name with contempt. *"It has to be her—a fucking security guard who lives in a shithole and pretends to be a cop."*

Terrance had heard of this sort of thing, he'd even seen a few of them on the freeway—men dressed as policeman, riding police bikes, pretending to be officers. *"I think it's a gay thing,"* Terrance thought to himself. He remembered seeing a movie somewhere of policemen having sex with each other. Their rough play frightened Terrance.

"That would explain it, although I didn't know the girls did it too. And yet, there's still the question of how she found me."

Terrance wondered if he'd ever been near one of those rough clubs or in any way might have been close to... *"Wait, wait, wait, oh my God, I remember the car, her car, the blue Crown Vic. It was parked by the sporting goods store on 75th the night I torched it. I remember it now. I thought it was a couple of kids getting loose, having sex, making out, but it must have been her doing weird, cop-type things, sleazing about in the dark—fuck, she must have seen me, followed me—that sneaky whore, that nasty churro-guarding cunt."*

Terrence ran his hand over his cut lip; his tongue did the same for his chipped tooth. *"Oh, she'll pay for this alright. I'm not sure how. But she is gonna pay."* He hurried back to his Fiesta, his ire rising. He'd get his revenge; but if he didn't get to work, he was going to be fired.

* * * * * * * * * * *

That night he neither watched nor burned. He sat patiently

and waited for her to arrive. At 2:45 a.m., her bullshit sedan skidded into the parking lot. She jumped out hot.

"What the hell are you doing? Why the fuck isn't that house on fire?"

"I'm sorry," Terrance lied. "I had no way to reach you. I needed help. I knocked over a box inside and I couldn't pick it up. I couldn't just leave it. They'd catch me and I'd lose my job. Please, I couldn't leave it. I need help please!"

"You fucking little worm," the bullshitter now known as Gina said. "I told you I needed it done. I'll bust your fucking..."

"No, I swear I'll do it," Terrance pleaded. "I want to do it; you know I do, just help me, there's still time if you help."

"Alright," Gina gave in. "What the fuck is it? What did you drop?"

"It's a box," Terrance said, "a big box. I couldn't lift it myself."

Terrance led the way into the storage units. The hallway was dark but as he cranked the timer switch, the overhead fluorescents sputtered to life. She followed him down the corridors, Terrance turning switches as he walked from hallway to hallway. It was a tight maze of wooden doors and Master locks.

"Wait." Terrance stopped in front of a door marked Men's and shyly motioned to his crotch. "I gotta pee, OK?"

"Are you fucking kidding me?" Gina asked. "You gotta go tinky? Fucking pathetic little bug. Hurry the fuck up!"

Terrance entered the bathroom and shut the door.

"Fuck her," he thought. *"She made me suck that gun, she's going to hurt me—this is her fault, not mine. She's the liar."*

He reached under the sink and grabbed a plastic bottle of Clorox and poured two fingers worth into an open tomato can that had been reserved for bathroom odds and ends—loose screws, knobs, etc.—the pouring bleach sounded like a masculine whizz. Terrance giggled.

"What the fuck are you doing in there?" Gina demanded.

"I'm sorry." Terrance lied, "I just peed on my shirt."

"Oh, for fucks sake. Come on!"

Terrance washed his hands and then for good measure, and extra protection, he grabbed the white, long-handled, toilet brush that was stored in a bucket by the john, and he opened the door.

"Come on," Gina said, "what took so…"

Terrance threw the bleach into her eyes. He dropped the can and jumped toward her, swinging the plastic brush. He connected a handle-bending blow to her head.

She screamed, clawing at her face, backing away from the blow. "My eyes, my fucking eyes!"

Terrance didn't let up; he swung again, the brush breaking over her arm—the plastic scrubbing head flying off, bouncing viciously and skidding down the hallway. Terrance stabbed her with the broken handle; the cheap dirty plastic digging into her chest.

"I'll kill you, you little fuck! I'll kill you!" Gina became crazed, an injured animal, fighting for her life. She swung blindly, advancing toward Terrance—who, by the way, had not envisioned things progressing like this. She took a wide swipe and tore his face with her nails. Terrance, terrified, turned and ran. Three hallways he traveled before he realized he was not being followed.

"Shit, shit, shit, shit," he said. *"This is bad. This is real bad."* He touched his face and flinched, pulling back fingers wet with clear ooze and blood. *"Oh, fuck! Listen to her!"*

Gina was pounding and screaming—a now blind assailant thrashing against the walls.

"I have to stop this!" Terrance thought.

Terrance checked his watch. He had time, but not much, something had to be done. He needed to be calm—a deep breath and a slow count to ten.

"One...two...three...okay, I need something harder, something that'll knock her out."

Terrance ran to the parking lot. He fished his keys from his pant's pocket and opened the trunk of his car. He retrieved a tire iron—a heavy, dirty, and slightly rusty, weapon of sorts. It would do. He ran back to the building and threw open the door. Gina was there! She had somehow made her way to the exit—her eyes swollen shut. She grabbed at Terrance. Terrance swung without thinking, a vicious tire-iron chop that landed brutally on her forehead. Gina's hands dropped immediately to her sides. She rag-dolled to the floor—blood pouring over her face and onto the concrete.

"Fuck..." Terrance stood—breathing hard, shaking as she unconsciously bled. He kicked her with his foot, no movement. He kicked again, still nothing—her eyes swollen and closed. He wasn't sure if she was dead, but she might be; it didn't look like she was breathing. Terrance took off his jacket and laid it over her face. He swung—a strong downward slash with the tire-iron—four solid blows he gave, each one undefended and well aimed.

Terrance stopped and dropped his weapon. It bounced off the concrete, clattered and lay still. She had to be dead. He had to work quickly. Terrance tucked the edges of the bloody jacket around her head—wrapping her like a broken, bloody present, and then he dashed off to find some better materials for the job. The day man would be here soon and this place was a mess. He had to tidy her up then square it away.

"Thank God I don't need help with that box," Terrance snickered.

There was a supply counter up front, not well stocked—this wasn't U-Haul after all, but there were some packing materials—tape, blanket pads, and bubble wrap. Terrance jumped the counter, grabbed a package of bubble wrap and a spool of "this is a real bitch to get off the roll" clear plastic tape—it would do.

Terrance was glad he'd wrapped her head. He didn't want to look at her. And now, other than the mess, it was just arms, legs and a trunk—not human at all. *"Jesus, I need her keys."* He patted down her pockets and found the keys. There was a purple rabbit's foot attached to the ring, and a hard plastic picture of some fat kid. He didn't look like her, at least as far as Terrence could remember, but Gina, much like the rabbit, had now been altered. He tore the bubble wrap out of the package, lifted her head and slid the plastic underneath. He then rolled her on to her side and pulled a full sheet about her before he wound the tape around. It wasn't hard, and the occasional popping bubble made it almost amusing. He struggled with the clear tape. Having no scissors or knife he attempted to tear it, but it was impossible, so he just kept wrapping until the roll was spent.

Terrance hustled outside, jumped in her car and backed it up to the door. Her car stunk, wild-mountain pine-berry or some car freshener scent—it was thick, sickeningly thick.

"Ha!" Terrance thought. *"It would be weeks before they smelled a body in here, if that was the plan…"* But it wasn't, it was just nice to know that if Terrance got lazy—which he wouldn't—he could leave that crazy bitch in here and they wouldn't smell her for weeks. He smiled—things were heading back to normal. He pulled the trunk latch and checked his watch. He had a solid hour before Tony, the day man, arrived—that is, if he showed up on time; he was supposed to be here at least 15 minutes before clock-in but he was always late.

Terrance hopped out of the car and darted back into Hedge's. He grabbed Gina by her feet and dragged her outside. She was heavy, but the occasionally popping bubble wrap helped her slide. He dragged her over to the back of the car, lifted the trunk lid and…

"What the fuck!" Terrance recoiled in horror. There she was, the young blonde, eyes wide open and staring blankly at Terrance— dead as could be.

"Oh, you nasty bitch." Terrance said, looking down at the bubble wrapped body. *"You nasty, nasty, bitch. What have you done? You killed her?"*

This wasn't going to be pleasant. He couldn't have that thing in the trunk starring at him as he loaded Gina in. It just wouldn't do. He ran back inside and grabbed a packing blanket from the store. *"Fuck, $10.99 for the blanket, $12 for the bubble wrap, $2 for the tape, this is getting ridiculous."*

He went back outside, pulled the blanket out of the pack, shook it twice, then held it in front of him and advanced blind on the trunk. He covered the young girl's body and then tucked the blanket around it. Gina was next. He pulled her over to a sitting position against the car and then he kind of stood her up, her back to the trunk. It was a bitch—she was dead weight. He had to slide her up and then push her back inside. The legs were easier. He lifted those up and just kind of folded her on top of herself. He stuffed her down and shut the lid. Terrance drove the car around the corner and parked it. It was too late to do what he needed to do and the car would be fine here. There was still blood on Hedge's floor and he needed to do a twice-over before he clocked out.

* * * * * * * * * * *

The next night Terrance arrived early to work—tired, but ready to go. He was disappointed, looking forward to torching that home, watching that young girl flame-dance through the window had been exciting, and now it'd come to this. He grabbed a large plastic gas can from his car—he loved gas, easy to come by, getting a touch expensive, but so much fun to work with, quick, easy and a smell that could bring even a drunken man back from a stupor. He walked around the corner. Her car was as he left it: legally parked, fully registered, and fresh as a pine-mountain daisy. He opened the trunk and poured gas over the bodies—the air-freshener was still overpowering. He shut the lid, unlocked the driver's door, put the keys in the ignition and liberally doused the interior with petrol before he locked up, leaving his red plastic gas container inside— they were cheap, and untraceable, as if there would be anything left to trace.

"This is a joke," Terrance thought, "a simple car job; a job for kids really. I should leave a yo-yo on the curb, but the police wouldn't get it."

Terrance pulled a lighter from his pocket and lit the end of a smoke—a nasty habit that he'd recently picked up—and thought about quitting, but the idea of never entertaining that cheery red smoke tip again was too sad to bear, so he took a long, thoughtful drag and gave up giving up.

He pulled a waxy piece of thick twine from his pocket, lit the end and tossed it into the pool of gas he'd spilt beneath the car. It ignited and the Crown Victoria was quickly consumed. Terrance turned his back and walked away. Cars never blew as fast as you see in the movies—it takes time, time and an experienced flame to get the right effect.

Terrance smiled, *"Yeah, this was a shit job, but there's a ripe house, Three-Thirty-Six Sand Canyon Drive, and it's waiting to burn. There's no sense in not fulfilling my promise to Gina. Of course, it's no longer occupied, so my* ménage à trois *will have to wait, but that neighborhood, a canvas fit for a master."*

The Evening Trees

The forest was a thousand lives old and the canopy of black sky that covered its boughs was held in place by a billion glittering stars. The Old Man stood on the edge of the wood gazing into the trees.

"Is there no way through?" he asked.

This question was directed to no one in particular, for he stood alone and, as far as his eyes could see, the forest ran a razor-sharp line through the world.

"How did I get here? I was home in my bed—my nightclothes are proof of that, and yet, I am here and without pain."

He ran his hands across his 80-year-old frame—slowly caressing his arms and chest. The dull, relentless ache that had plagued his days was gone. He no longer felt tired. He wanted to tell his children that he was better, on the mend, wanting to walk the beach again, but he was alone—alone with a forest that appeared impenetrable. He reached out and touched the trunk of one of the trees. Its bark, if you could call it that, was smooth as human flesh stretched over bone—scarred and tanned to a deep winter brown. There was something familiar there, a wave of memory that came upon him, and would have assailed him, if he had let his hand stay. He took a deep, younger man's breath and reached out again. A solitary wolf howled in the distance. He held his palm firmly against the tree's flesh, and braced himself for the onslaught…

…Their shouts were in sharp contrast to the soft, blue, blanket that he was wrapped in. He was a newborn, held in her arms and, at times, without thinking, she squeezed him harder than she should have. She was screaming—her words in knife-tumbling flight at the target of her anger…a vanquished military man. "You're a loser," she screamed, "you don't care about our baby, about me, about anything. I fucking hate you, and I hate this!" She recklessly held the child aloft. "You're a cheat, and a liar, and I wish he'd never been born."

The Old Man removed his hand from the tree. He was that child—a tug-of-war witness to an argument between his parents. He was the fruit of his father's reckless lust and his mother's demented anger. He wasn't wanted.

As far as he could remember there'd been hostility in his childhood home; and why his parents stayed together, he never knew. He'd never seen them show affection—or anything resembling love. He had once walked in on them having sex—the military man ship-shaped and squared away on top of a theatrically submissive woman—her moans and faked "no" protestations giving cadence to his thrusts, but it wasn't love. In fact, to the Old Man's six-year-old eyes, it was ugly and violent.

It was strange, thinking of them now, in this foreign place. He hadn't thought of his parents in years—and he never remembered them looking as they did—his mother, even in her fury, so young and beautiful, and his father, handsome and proud in his uniform. When was the last time he'd seen them? His father had died of a heart attack when he was still a boy, and his mother had been gone some thirty years now. The last time he saw her she hadn't recognized him, and she was angry at his inability to stop the winter snow from filling her bedroom.

The Old Man sat on the ground, not frustrated, but unsure of how to proceed. It was then that she walked from the forest. He recognized her instantly, although her face changed with each step she took. She was his first wife, and then his youngest daughter, his last love, and then she became his eldest. She shimmered and shifted across the grass until she stood before him, a masque of all the women he had ever loved.

"It's good to see you again," she said, her kind tones comforting, reassuring. "You look well—older though, yes?" She smiled, the smile of his broken heart, but he felt safe and whole by her side.

"I'm not sure where I am," he said, "or what I'm to do. Do you know?"

The woman lowered herself to the ground and reclined on the grass. She wore a gown of sheer white, the naked lines of her body visible beneath the cloth, her light brown hair falling in long, soft, curls toward the ground.

"You never get tired of looking to me for answers, do you?"

She was right; he'd always trusted the counsel of women, more so than he had men; his manager, his editor, and his best friend, all women—benevolent feminine angels. He was attracted by their strength and their kindness—although, when it came to lovers, he usually fell for the domineering, unstable, unfaithful type—the opposite of what he craved.

"There is a path for you." She gestured toward the trees and where there had been none, an entrance now appeared into the woods. "You love to walk and you'll find nothing in that forest that hasn't already hurt you."

She touched his forehead and brushed the ghost of his hair from his eyes.

"Do you know where I am?" he said.

"Yes. You're in bed, at home. Some of us are by your side. Your daughters, Ana and Georgia, walked down to the cove; they're getting to know each other again. Your friend Julia is on the phone to your agent, and your manager is in the garden, crying, and talking to the press—you really had been quite the naughty boy, hadn't you?" She ran the back of her hand across his cheek and then lightly touched his lips.

"And my mother and my father," he asked, "why?"

"I think you need to see," she said.

"Am I dead?"

"No," she replied, "not yet, but soon we hope."

The Old Man began to cry. There were times that he'd wanted to die—a few half-hearted suicide attempts, more out of frustration than sincerity—but in his later years he'd come to appreciate life, and now he selfishly clung to it.

"Come," she said.

She pulled him to his feet and then into her arms. "I've always loved you and I'm sorry that you could never feel it."

She walked him toward the entrance to the woods, guiding his steps. He followed like a child. He was a large man, a man who in his younger years intimidated and bullied other men, but he had always felt smaller when a woman was involved. They walked to the edge of the forest and he waited to follow her in.

"I'm not going with you," she said. "This time, you go alone."

"Why?" he asked.

"Because you need to see what was hidden—what you refused to see in life."

He walked into the cool evening shade—the trees closed about him.

* * * * * * * * * * *

The woods were dark, but not unpleasant; they reminded him of a theatre, an empty house with the lights down, the trees were seats occupied by the unseen memories of his life. He walked down the wooded aisle.

The Old Man was expecting his touch to release the past, but as he walked, he ran his hands along the trees and received no thoughts to disturb him. The forest began to glow—a gentle light filling the space ahead. He heard the sounds of a playground—school-age children yelling with delight, laughing and extoling the glee of their days. Suddenly, the laughter turned vicious…

"It's a fight!" They yelled, "a fight!" The children were chanting, cheering on a recess battle with wild grade school yells. He moved closer. And now he was upon them, and among them. The children were standing in a circle blocking his view, the crowd jostling back and forth, side to side, fringing the disturbance. They paid him no notice as he pushed forward; stepping into the group, trying to see what he knew he must. He was transported into the scene, cut and scraped by falling hard on grade school blacktop…

… A bigger boy—a lunchtime bully had pushed him to the ground, teasing him for his too large hand-me-down pants and his older brother's shirt. He tried to get to his feet but he was brutally kicked between the legs. In an effort to distance themselves from the violence, his Cheerios and nonfat breakfast milk escaped his stomach—the liquid, as it hit the pavement, retained its watered-down bluish tint. The children cheered his attacker. Cowering on

the ground he saw nothing but shoes—P.F. Flyers, All Stars, and Wallabys—dancing and stepping to the beat of the bully's blows.

"Help me!" he pleaded to the crowd. "Help!"

His cries were met with jeers and screams. Only the blows came forward, and they, in succession, unmercifully falling. "Help me!" he screamed. "Please!"

He heard a woman's voice over the yells—familiar, pushing her way through the throng. "Let me through," she ordered, "let me through."

The children parted and from his place on the ground, he saw her shoes—his mother's cheap JC Penney pumps—and for a moment he thought he was saved as the bully's blows ceased. He raised his head toward her, the woman who gave him birth, but before his eyes could meet hers they traveled the lines of her face and nothing in that journey said comfort. She wore the same contorted angry cheering lines that the children's faces held—and noting her fury, he knew there would be no sanctuary. His mother joined the chants. "Hit him!" she cried. "Hit him back!"

The children who at first were held at bay by the grown-up presence now renewed their anger, and the bully reared his fist back and fired a connecting no-help shot to his mouth. He was knocked cold.

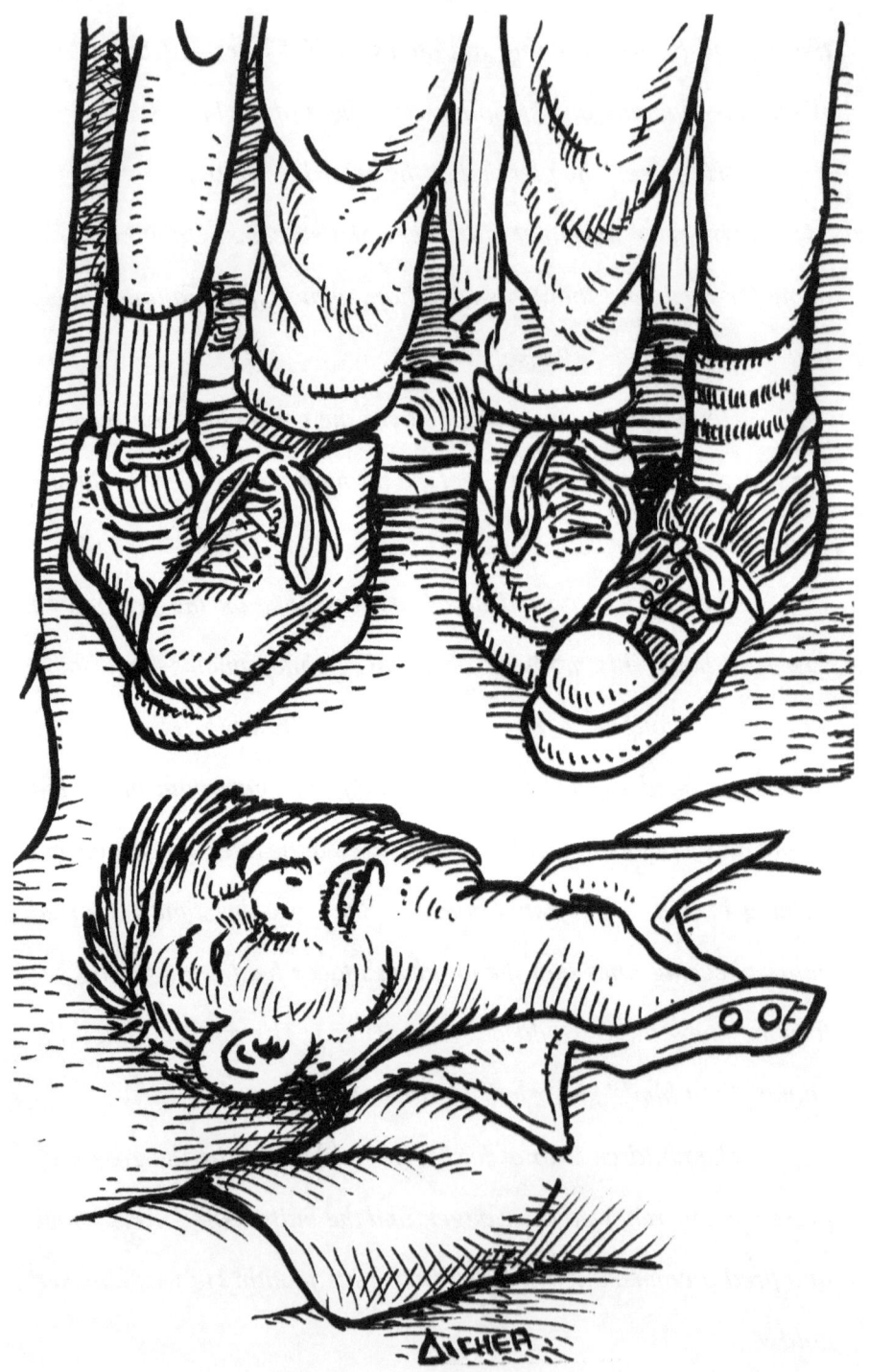

When he awoke he was sitting with his back against a tree. The children were gone. He could hear his mother's pumps furiously marching off through the forest, but as his head cleared, the woods grew quiet. He touched his face, expecting dried blood and missing teeth, but he was whole. He was as unencumbered with physical pain as he was when he began, but his heart was heavy. He remembered that day, and that beating, and the look on his mother's face as she refused his pleas. She thought she was helping him— encouraging him to be strong. She was wrong. He was a gentle child and wished no harm on others. He had counted on her to save him, to come to his aid, love, and protect him, but, as always, he would be disappointed.

That was the last time he was ever beaten by another boy. He grew strong and the words *'hit him'* had filled his insides until his anger had blossomed like vicious flowers across his knuckles. Throughout his life, he had left a trail of beaten boys and men, all unknowing victims of his mother's twisted love. Strangely, he had never wanted to hurt the men he fought. He felt sorry for them as they quailed beneath his blows. Somewhere under the hate instilled was that gentle boy cowering in a soft corner of his soul. But that isn't to say that he wasn't vicious, because he had been. He'd been called a monster, a sociopath, soulless, and maybe at times that was true—but his actions were only an offering to the cruel childhood Goddess that he'd adored.

The Old Man stood and headed in the direction of his mother's echoing footsteps. He had no idea if the way was true, but the forest made itself hospitable to his path. As he walked, his thoughts drifted to his second wife—a woman cold of heart and withdrawn from his love. She was so much like his mother; not in looks—her blonde hair and light blue eyes were in sharp contrast to his mother's brown on brown, but in the way she loved, or rather, the love she withheld. There was a wall of distance around her that he could never breach no matter how hard he tried. Many days he acted as a willful child would, for it seemed that in her anger toward him, a slight connection was made, but she soon grew tired of his games and she further withdrew.

She'd been verbally accosted that day. Two twenty-something punks had thrown bargain-bin comments toward her ass as she walked past them into a shop. He was waiting for her in the car— she was to be quick, only a few items. He witnessed their exchange and did nothing. When his wife returned, she berated him for his unwillingness to act.

"What's the matter with you?" she demanded. "Didn't you hear what they said?"

"I thought it would be best to let it go." He was confused. She knew that he'd been working with a counselor—trying to reach the bottom of his rage. She shouldn't encourage this.

"You're a fucking coward, and you don't defend me."

She turned her back to him as they drove through the parking lot. He could picture her cold gaze freezing the windows of cars as they passed. He turned out and pulled up to a red light.

"That's them," she said, pointing at the two black-haired punks who were now casually driving away. He looked across her and saw them. They were stopped in the left turn lane, oblivious—an unsuspecting red Volkswagen getting ready to pull onto the highway. His mother was now in the passenger seat of his car, although she was clothed in the bleached blond hair and plastic-titted body of his wife.

"You're a coward," she said. The cold indifference in her voice triggered something inside. He yanked the wheel hard to the left, cut across traffic, and blocked the Volkswagen from proceeding. He was out of the car before she could protest—or encourage. The driver's window was down and before the driver knew what was *coming; his head was slammed back into the headrest with a see-what-I-am punch to the face. It was immediately followed by a series of vicious blows delivered cold, but in hot procession one after another. The driver went unconscious, bleeding. The surrounding cars were honking now and he could hear screaming, muffled, coming over his shoulder. It was not unlike the children's voices from the playground, although these screams were not egging him on.*

"Police!" they yelled. "Call the police!"

He slowed down and dimly became aware of what he was doing. The incident became a violent black marmalade dream that slowed his motion, dragging his actions to a standstill. The driver was barely lucid, moaning in his seat—the other boy, running terrified away. He walked back to his car and got in. The image of his mother was gone. His passenger was once again his wife, and his defense of her honor had softened her none. They divorced shortly thereafter.

He walked on.

The ground was soft beneath his feet, a path of branch and fallen leaf. He inhaled and was comforted by the strong scent of pine and decaying brush—it would have been a pleasant walk but for the memories. And yet, he now knew where his violence began. He'd done years of therapy, the counselors word-dancing around the influence of his mother, but he had never seen it as clearly as he did this day. The old schoolyard memory had lain silent until now, and his connection between the two had somehow freed him—*you did this, because of this*. It was so elementary in its simplicity and yet the rage he'd carried from a grade school recess had traveled some seventy years through his life. He checked himself—ran through a few various scenarios in his head—incidences where he might seek a violent solution to the situation—and it was as if the pathway of aggression had disappeared from his mind. He could now see only peaceful, loving resolution.

There was a light growing before him, it was a midmorning yellow glow. His feet were no longer sinking into dirt. He was shuffling across the stained yellowed linoleum of his youth. Cheap floor tiles were spread along the path as he walked into the kitchen of his boyhood home.

"WHAT ARE YOU DOING?" It was his mother. She was dressed in a short blue nightgown and nothing else. Her hair was undone, loose and uncontrolled—her eyes matched.

The Old Man recognized the memory. He was in 7th grade

and should've been in class.

"Why aren't you in school?" his mother asked. "What are you doing home?"

He supplied as much of an answer as he did some years ago...none.

"I said, WHAT ARE YOU DOING!" Anger flushed her skin.

"I didn't go," he replied. "I didn't feel like it."

"You didn't feel like it?" she said. "Do you feel like this?" His mother gestured to herself—a "Valley of the Dolls" wanna-be. "Do you feel like making me hurt?" She punched herself in the face.

"No!" he screamed. "Mom! Don't!"

She hit herself again—harder this time—closed fisted blows knocking the false lashes from her eyes. She screamed and flailed her arms. "Look at me! Look at what you're doing to me."

"I'm sorry!" he yelled. "I won't...I'll go to school! I promise!"

She moved possessed across the kitchen floor—a broken mother-toy unwound. She swept her arm across the kitchen counter sending dirty plates and glasses crashing to the floor.

"LOOK AT ME! YOU DO THIS TO ME!"

She fell to the ground, her arm cut and bleeding; her eyes

now still but rolled back beneath sky blue Maybelline lids. She lay

sobbing—nightgown clenched high above her waist—exposed.

    "Mom? Please," he begged her. "I'm sorry."

    No response.

He walked over to her, bent down, and straightened the nightgown over her legs. He gently touched her arm. "Mom?" he asked, as if she was someone else. "Are you okay?"

She released a low sorrowful moan—the sound of an animal injured on the highway—a voice somewhere below human.

"Should I call Dad?"

No answer.

He grabbed the hard plastic phone off the wall and rotary dialed his father's work. He was surprised he remembered the number after all these years. The secretary who answered was not pleased—his father was low man at the company and wasn't to be taking calls.

"What's going on?" his father said.

There was no, "Hello," or, "Are you okay?" It was strictly business, "God-damn-my-fucked-up-kid."

"It's Mom. She's not all right."

"What happened?" It was an order, not a question. "Where is she?"

"She's on the floor crying. She won't get up. She hurt herself."

"What did you do to her?"

"I didn't go to school. I..."

"God damn it! What the fuck did you do to her?"

He hung up the phone before the question came again, "What did *you* do to *her*?"

When he turned back to his mother, she was gone. The broken glass on the floor began to shine. The forest glade returned and the bright pieces of the memory became the dappled sunlight on fallen leaves.

His mother had been ill—depressed and untreated. His father, in an attempt to gain control of the situation, had blamed him—he was the easy out.

"Fuck." He swore to no one but himself.

His first wife was unstable—wild and dangerous. She cut herself when she was upset—torn scissor flesh held as a testament to how he hurt her—*if only he hadn't done this, if only he hadn't said that*. He catered to her illness, babied her, and at times made love to her as the fresh cuts on her arm still bled. She was his mother. Immediately he recognized himself as Oedipus and was sickened by the thought, but it was true. In his teen years he'd battled his father—toe-to-toe in violent front-yard stand-offs, and the heart attack that ultimately claimed his father's life, well, he was blamed for the stress that he had laid on the man. He inadvertently had killed his father.

Deep into the night he followed the path, yet no new memories came. It was as if the forest wanted him to ponder what he'd learned—to slowly chew the pain of truth until it filled his soul. Wolves of self-pity howled in the distance.

"Why me? I was a child. I didn't deserve this. I only wanted her love—their love."

He was tired. He didn't want to continue. He didn't want to feel anymore. He wanted to rest, but instead he moved on.

All of them, he thought, *those lovers who stood in her stead—surrogate mothers just as sick as his own—a sad, chorus line of cold, unstable women—women that, try as he might, he could not help. They would never love or support him as he wished. He'd searched for that perfect love, but he never found it, because the world, in which he searched, wasn't populated by his dreams, but by the reality of his pain. And yet, he had been surrounded by kind, loving women who adored him. They hated the choices he'd made, the pain he'd put himself through as he unknowingly sought to heal his first love, his mother, by attempting to save those sick women he chose. His friends and his daughters watched him fail, and they loved him all the more for his unwillingness to give up, to walk away, and to turn his back on those that he thought needed his love most.*

He felt something brush against his hip. It was a wolf—a large grey walking beside him. He was not afraid.

"You're part of me," the Old Man said. "I knew you when I heard your voice in the trees. You prey on the weak—your hunger, insatiable."

The wolf watched his face as he talked.

"All my life you've followed me, waiting for me to succumb to the poison that she planted—and you were close. I felt your foul breath against my neck and your scent upon the razor that I took to my wrist, but this forest has stripped the sheep's wool from my eyes, and the anger from my heart. I'm no meal to you now. I'm free."

The forest opened onto a beach. The wolf disappeared and the Old Man walked out onto the sand. There were bodies of men, women and children lying in a lifeless pile—thousands of bodies.

* * * * * * * * * * *

"He's awake." It was his youngest daughter's voice.

He was lying in his bed; his body racked with pain—heavy, hard to breathe, but he felt them near—the human angels who had loved him.

"Father," his eldest spoke. "You can let go, Dad. We're here.

We love you." She squeezed his hand.

"I'm so sorry," he whispered. "I'm sorry that I hurt you. I just wanted their love—I wanted *her* love. I tried to heal those who could not be healed. I put you aside and gave them love that was rightfully yours. Please forgive me, my dears. You have always held my heart."

"And we have always loved you, father."

He closed his eyes.

Onto the pile of bodies he climbed. They were stacked toward the stars—thousands of the dead—a flesh stairway to the heavens. Lighter he grew as he rose, until he became so light that he stepped from his body and into the night.

MORE PUNK HOSTAGE PRESS BOOKS

Fractured (2012) by Danny Baker

A. Razor
Better Than A Gun In A Knife Fight (2012)
Drawn Blood: Collected Works From D.B.P.LTD., 1985-1995 (2012)
Beaten Up Beaten Down (2012)
Small Catastrophes In A Big World (2012)
Half-Century Status (2013).
Days Of Xmas Poems (2014)
Puro Purismo (2021)

Iris Berry
The Daughters Of Bastards (2012)
All That Shines Under The Hollywood Sign (2019)

Impress (2012) by C.V. Auchterlonie

Tomorrow, Yvonne - Poetry & Prose For Suicidal Egoists (2012)
by Yvonne De la Vega

Miracles Of The Blog: A Series (2012) by Carolyn Srygley- Moore

8th & Agony (2012) by Rich Ferguson

Jack Grisham
Untamed (2013)
Code Blue: A Love Story ~ Limited Edition (2014)
Code Blue: The Hide Under the Mattress Edition (2020)

Dennis Cruz
Moth Wing Tea (2013)
The Beast Is We (2018)

Blood Music (2013) by Frank Reardon

Showgirl Confidential (2013) by Pleasant Gehman

Yeah, Well... (2014) by Joel Landmine

MORE PUNK HOSTAGE PRESS BOOKS

Stealing The Midnight From A Handful Of Days (2014)
by Michele McDannold

History Of Broken Love Things (2014) by SB Stokes

Dreams Gone Mad With Hope (2014) by S.A. Griffin

How To Take A Bullet And Other Survival Poems (2014) by Hollie Hardy

Dead Lions (2014) by A.D. Winans

Nadia Bruce-Rawlings
Scars (2014)
Driving in the Rain (2020)

*WHEN I WAS A DYNAMITER, Or, how a Nice Catholic Boy Became a Merry
Prankster, a Pornographer, and a Bridegroom Seven Times* (2014)
by Lee Quarnstrom.

Alexandra Naughton
I Will Always Be Your Whore/Love Songs For Billy Corgan (2014)
*You Could Never Objectify Me More Than I've Already Objectified
Myself* (2015)

No Parachutes To Carry Me Home (2015) by Maisha Z Johnson

#1 Son And Other Stories (2017) by Michael Marcus

LOOKING FOR JOHNNY, The Legend of Johnny Thunders (2018)
by Danny Garcia

Burden Of Concrete (2020) by William S. Hayes

Dillinger's Thompson (2020) by Todd Moore

$100-A-Week Motel (2021) by Dan Denton

*My Life With the Dwarves: How I Drank, Fought and Fucked
My Way Around The World* (2021) by Vadge Moore